Robert Du Pontavice de Heussey

Villiers de l'Isle Adam

His life and works

Robert Du Pontavice de Heussey

Villiers de l'Isle Adam
His life and works

ISBN/EAN: 9783337409579

Printed in Europe, USA, Canada, Australia, Japan

Cover: Foto ©Raphael Reischuk / pixelio.de

More available books at **www.hansebooks.com**

VILLIERS de l'Isle ADAM

HIS LIFE AND WORKS

from the French of

Vicomte Robert du Pontavice de Heussey

By Lady Mary Loyd

London

William Heinemanr

MDCCCXCIV

TO
THE EVER BLESSED MEMORY
OF THE UNKNOWN INDIVIDUAL
WHO FIRST INTRODUCED ME TO
THE KNOWLEDGE OF THE FRENCH LANGUAGE,
THIS TRANSLATION
IS GRATEFULLY DEDICATED
BY MARY LOYD.

TO THE READER.

THE writings of Villiers de l'Isle Adam are so little known in this country, that it may not be out of place, before the adventurous reader embarks on the perusal of the following recollections, to endeavour, in the most cursory manner, to give some details concerning them.

The most stinging satire and the most radiant fancy; the keenest appreciation of nature, especially in her gloomier and more mysterious moods, and a constant endeavour to enforce the immutable truths of religion and morality, and the inevitable results of their contravention, run through all his stories. And nothing more genuinely witty can be imagined than some of his sketches viii TO THE READER.

of the more peculiarly Bohemian side of
Parisian life. The characteristic of Villiers'
work which must strike the thoughtful student most, is its magnificent thoroughness.
Every one of his tales bears the impress, not
only of laborious preparation, but of the most
conscientious elaboration. So that every
word, as it finally stands, is indispensable to
the true comprehension of the author's meaning. And this meaning, again, is almost
always of the highest; the satire, grave or gay,
good-humoured or severe, always tending to
the support of what is true and noble, and to
the punishment (or, at all events, the dis-
countenance) " of wickedness and vice."

The poet's immediate friends may have
blamed and deplored the extreme Bohemian-
ism into which his needy circumstances drove
him. We, who inherit the result of his life-
work—a work accomplished in the face of
constant difficulty and discouragement—can
have no room for any feeling but admiration
for the man who never published a line without giving it the highest polish he was capable
of imparting.

No modern writer, with the exception, perhaps, of Edgar Poe, whom Villiers so passionately admired, has his power of *dignifying the horrible.* And none, I believe (not even Pierre Loti, that master of the art of portraying nature, to the extent of making his readers actually feel the heat of the sun and the damp of the fog he describes), excels him in calling up, and in the fewest words, the beauty of an autumn sunset, the dreariness of a wild winter night, the horror of a long corridor in one of the prisons of the Spanish Inquisition,[1] or the exotic bloom of certain phases of existence in Paris.[2] Brevity, they say, is the soul of wit. Truly, in this case, brevity is the strength of style, and it is not easy, on a first perusal, to realize the concentrated power this same well-considered brevity gives to that of Villiers de l'Isle Adam.

Of his life I will say nothing. Its story is unfolded in the pages which succeed this

[1] "La Torture par l'Espérance."
[2] "Le Convive des dernières Fêtes," "Antonia," "L'Enjeu."

note.   A sad enough story it is, full of
struggle and failure, of brilliant hopes and
bitter deceptions.   The history of a great
soul, full of that peculiar simplicity and un-
fitness for coping with everyday cares which
so often accompany genius; and with that
sad and too common close, so eternally dis-
honouring to the public which turns a deaf
ear to the living charmer, charm he never so
wisely—death in an hospital ward, followed
by pæans of admiration when the brave
heart that had vainly ached for just one
responsive throb was stilled in the silence
of the grave.

There is a growing interest among cultivated people on this side of the Channel in
the extraordinary development of literature
in its most brilliant form on the other, and
I feel convinced that this sketch of the life
and works of one who, neglected and de-
preciated as he was to within a few months
of his premature death by all but a select
few, is now acclaimed as one of the chief
glories of modern literary France, will be
heartily welcomed by the many sympathetic

English admirers of our gifted neighbours, and that the knowledge they may thereby acquire of the great French writer's life and labour will inspire them with a desire to become acquainted with the remarkable group of tales, plays, and novels on which his reputation rests.

MARY LOYD.

In Memoriam.

THE author of the following recollections has passed into the silent country while the sheets of this translation were being prepared for the press. The thought that his book was about to be presented to the English public helped to cheer the last months of a long and trying illness. And to that public I submit these pages, in the confident belief that those who have the patience to read them will share my admiration for the graceful talent of their author, and will regret with me that one who might yet, if he had been spared, have done much invaluable work in literature and literary research, should have been cut off prematurely, "in the flower of his days."

Requiescat in Pace.

CONTENTS.

CHAPTER I.

CHAPTER II.

b

CHAPTER III.

CHAPTER IV.

CHAPTER V.

CHAPTER VI.

CHAPTER VII.

CHAPTER VIII.

CHAPTER IX.

CHAPTER X.

CHAPTER XI.

CHAPTER XII.

CHAPTER XIII.

CHAPTER XIV.

CHAPTER XV.

CHAPTER XVI.

Mon bien cher poète,.

— Et votre santé?.. J'espère qu'elle s'est
éclaircie.— À votre place,' je me porterais comme
un ou plusieurs monts-blancs:— Mais baste..
Je suis sûr qu'à cette heure, vous ne décrive
qu'une soixante douzième partie d'éclopés:
toutefois,.. si vous venez à partir pour
la grande nuit, vous aurez, ayez l'obligeance
de me prévenir afin que je compose,
pour votre gloire, et pour l'ébaudissure
de tous, quelque fantaisie funèbre en
mi bémol: c'est du meilleur ton: et
cela me poserait. —.
Je n'ai point reçu de lettre de mon
intéressante famille:.. Seurément et
moi, nous sommes dans la pauvreté;
ce qui fait que malgré tout mon bon
vouloir, je remets à quelques jours, si vous le

permettez, le remboursement de votre charmant
service : — ne me maudissez pas, il n'y
a pas de ma faute ; et je publie partout
vos louanges, — et votre urbanité. —
D'ailleurs, c'est votre faute : cela vous
apprendra à rendre service ; — je vous
demande un peu, si, au dix neuvième siècle,
il est permis de prêter de l'argent à ses
amis !— vous voulez donc qu'on vous
montre au doigt, quand vous entrerez dans
un salon ! — Je vous dénoncerai comme
coupable de lèse-égoïsme, à la société
moderne ; — cela vous sera bien ennuyeux ;
mais, voilà ce que c'est. —

— Les épreuves de master berrix, sont
du dernier comique : Leménant et moi
nous avons fait plusieurs gorges chaudes
en les apercevant. — Je vais lui écrire
une petite épître goguenarde qui lui
fatiguera le cervelet. — voici un échantillon
de sa manière : — tout est de cette façon :

{ L'vſaige de Don Jvan & deſ pêchevrſ du golfe

{ L'image de Don Juan et ses pêcheurs du golfe,

Voilà, dans un vers impossible, s'imprimer
de cet homme. ⌐

C'est une plaisanterie un peu trop chargé,
est-ce pas ? Entre nous, il faut être toqué,
pour avoir eu cette idée là. — Vous figurez
vous bien un volume de cette force sur
papier jaune ! Le mênant dit que sera
phosphorescent. — Le fait est que c'est
drôle, et que, dans mes œuvres complètes,
un jour, si j'ai jamais des œuvres complètes,
{ je pourrais me donner ce spectacle : quand
{ à présent, — Zut ! Je définis ainsi Bérain
C'est le nec plus ultrà grimaçant d'une typographie
surannée, — ou, si vous préférez, c'est le grattoir
mystique de la presse guttembergiesque : —
autrement dit le tombeau de l'édité ! ! —

Maintenant passons à des choses moins aléatoires.
Montfort est une ville, ou plutôt... ni je dis bien,
une ville, — pleine de boue et de calme. —

Nous y vivons, sous les ailes joyeuses de ce vieux
séraphin, qu'on appelle la gaieté. —

Ce pays pullule d'honnêtes gens : c'est à ne pas s'y
reconnaître, quand on vient de Paris. —

Il y a un moulin, un moulin pour de vrai,
absolument, comme dans les tableaux de Rosa
Bonheur, (nature morte) — Le mérant déverse
quotidiennement à la fenêtre son speech dévot
et son spleen métaphysico-transcendantal. Les
passants, effarés et rares, l'écoutent

——————————— l'écoutent.... et accompagnent
ses discours sur l'air : il a des boll. boll, boll !
Ce qui produit un effet, pour lequel je.
Ce congratule vivement. — Nous demeurons
sur la place, ce qui triple l'intérêt du
coup d'œil. — Moi, je rime paisiblement, au
milieu des tumultes. —

À bientôt, cher et aimable poète,
recevez l'assurance de mes sentiments
d'amitié la plus simple et la plus vraie.

Je vous serre la main et vous embrasse
de cœur. — rassurez moi sur votre santé
si vous avez le temps. —

Villiers de L'Isle-Adam

VILLIERS DE L'ISLE ADAM.

CHAPTER I.

First meeting—Family ties—Illustrious origin of Villiers
—Genealogy of the family of L'Isle Adam—The old
Emigrés—Good King Louis XVIII. and M. de
Villiers—Motto and coat-of-arms of the family—
The Curé of Ploumilliau—Villiers at the parsonage—
"L'Intersigne"—His Parents—Genealogy of the De
Carforts—Aunt Kerinou—Peculiarities of the Mar-
quis de l'Isle Adam—His golden dream—The
inheritance seeker—The treasure seeker.

ONE Thursday morning in November, 1858, I was in the dining-
room of my father's house at
Fougères. I was eating my sad
and solitary luncheon under the eye of a cross
old nurse; and my heart swelled as I looked

at the cheerful winter sun outside the window
panes, and thought of my brothers, more
fortunate than myself, who were frolicking
through the leafless woods which so pictu-
resquely crown the village of St. Germain.
There my grandfather lived, in an old manor-
house amongst the trees, and every Thursday, according to custom, my family spent the
day with him. This time I had been left
behind, as a punishment for some childish
misdemeanour or some ill-learnt lesson.

Suddenly I heard the rumble of a carriage
on the rough pavement of our street, generally as silent as the grave, and soon I saw a
hired chaise stop before our windows. I
know not why my heart began to beat so fast
when the bell (pulled by a vigorous hand)
clanged noisily. A moment after, the door
of the dining-room opened, and a fair young
man with a large head, and wrapped in rich
furs, rushed in like a whirlwind. He vaulted
lightly over the table at which I was sitting,
and lifting me up, before I had recovered
from my astonishment, he kissed me heartily,
saying, " Good day, my little man—you don't

know me! I am your cousin Matthias!"
But I did know him well! For long he had
filled my childish imagination, haunted already
by the demon of literature. How often had
I listened open-mouthed, forgetful of my
plate, while my father recounted at the family
board the adventures, the oddities, the traits
of genius of Cousin Matthias! True, I understood but vaguely what my father meant,
but it had for me all the mysterious charm of
the unknown. Meanwhile the unexpected
guest had asked for food, having come straight
from Paris, without warning, as was his way.
I see him now, opposite me, eating heartily,
asking me questions, laughing at my prattle
(he had put me at my ease at once), and stopping every now and then to push back with
his hand a thick lock of fair hair which kept
falling over his eyes.

"You know," said he to my astounded
attendant, "I am off to St. Germain, the little
chap with me. When *I* come, all punish-
ments are stopped."

Willy nilly, she had to wrap me in my
cloak and comforter! Ten minutes later

Cousin Matthias and I, seated in the little hired gig, were bowling along the frosty road which led from the town of Fougères to the village of St. Germain.

Such was my first never-to-be-forgotten meeting with Philip Augustus Matthias de Villiers de l'Isle Adam, then in all the bloom of his youth and the first blush of his wonderful genius—his brow and eyes radiant with those beautiful illusions, those glorious dreams, which attended his entrance into life, which never abandoned him in his saddest hours, and whose melancholy phantoms hovered over the hospital bed on which he died, high-spirited to the last, hopeful and resigned.

As has been seen, our families were kin. But I think that the cousinship between Villiers and my father, and later, by inheritance, between Villiers and myself, was more intellectual than anything else. The family bond which unites us seems to me very slight. It should be sought, I think, in the alliance of both our families with that of De Kersauson. But that is little matter. What is far more

urgent is to establish the absolutely incontestable nobility of the origin of the great
writer. In his lifetime a sort of mysterious
legendary haze gathered round his personality,
and I fancy he rather enjoyed deepening the
fog. At all events, such was his hatred of
all that was conventional, that his Titanic
dreams became historical facts concerning
which he would admit of no discussion. All
those who have heard him speak of his ancestors, of their riches, of " the stately sea-
beaten manor-house," in which his early
youth was passed, will understand, without
further insisting, what I mean. Yet, in those
rare, and for him, wearisome moments, when
he returned to earth, Villiers knew his family
history perfectly, and in its minutest detail.
He had studied the subject profoundly, and
his genius illuminated for him all that was
prosaic and dull in provincial and Parisian
archives. I know a certain work of his,
dealing with the life of the Maréchal de
Villiers de l'Isle Adam, which is a masterpiece of clearness, eloquent expression, and
erudition. I will return to it at a more

opportune moment.   At present I am chiefly concerned with the poet's origin.

The illustrious family of Villiers de l'Isle Adam, Seigneurs de Villiers de l'Isle Adam and de Chailly, originated in the Ile de France.   Several knights of the name took part in the Crusades, others occupied the highest positions about the court and in the army.   In fact, the brilliant name of Villiers de l'Isle Adam is constantly flashing across the pages of our history.   But the most cele- brated amongst these great noblemen, too well known for me to add anything to what has already been written concerning them, are, in order of date : Pierre, who was Grand- master and Porte Oriflamme of France in 1355;   Jean, Marshal of France in 1437; and Philippe, Grand Master of the Order of the Knights of Malta, the heroic defender of the Island of Rhodes against Suliman in 1521.   The nephew of this last, François, Marquis de Villiers de l'Isle Adam, was " Grand Louvetier de France " in 1550.   The grandson of François married, about 1670, a daughter of the old house of De Courson, and settled in the bishopric of St. Brieuc, where he founded the Breton branch of the Villiers de l'Isle Adam family. The grandson of this last, a lieutenant in the Royal Navy, married in his turn, in 1780, a Mdlle. de Kersauson. At the time of the Revolution, he emigrated to England with his family. And here should be related an incident which has an important bearing on the curious lawsuit brought by Villiers against the descendants of the comedian Lockroy, an action of which I shall give the details when I come to that part of the poet's life in which it occurred.

At the time of the Revolution the house of De l'Isle Adam had greatly declined from its ancient splendour. I will not go into the causes of this change; suffice it to say, that when the naval officer emigrated with those belonging to him, his income barely sufficed for the strictest necessaries of life. It follows, that once established abroad, he did not for some time attempt to return. Meanwhile, the Bourbons having returned to France, all the so-called servants of the august exiles were clamouring for the reward of their services.

A certain Mons. de Villiers Deschamps, a rich man, and an excellent royalist, asked permission to revive the name of De l'Isle Adam, which he affirmed to be completely extinct, and to which a distant relationship gave him a claim. Good Louis XVIII., delighted with a petition which would cost him nothing but a signature, granted without hesitation the prayer of his loyal subject. Thus it came about, that until the day when its luxurious peace was disturbed by the poet's inopportune interference, the family of De Villiers, all unconscious of the fraud, bore an illustrious name and a famous coat-of-arms to which it had no earthly title.

As I have spoken of the arms of the De Villiers, this may be the proper place to describe them : " D'or au chef d'azur chargé d'un dextrochère vêtu d'un fanon d'hermines." Mottoes : " Va oultre ! " and also " La main à l'œuvre."

All those familiar with Villiers de l'Isle Adam and his wonderful books, will recognize that these two proud mottoes seem to have been made for him.

" Va oultre ! " " Go forward ! "   This is what
he always did.   His clear, prophetic glance
piercing the heavens, and reaching in its
impetuous and aspiring flight far beyond the
horizon of ordinary human thought! " La
main à l'œuvre ! " " Hand at work ! "   Yes,
ceaselessly at work, even in the darkest hours
of misery, that hand of the artist and the
gentleman, at once so delicate and so brave,
whose labour only rested in death ! In his
last days he used to watch, sadly enough, the
failing strength of those poor brave hands
which could no longer hold the pen, and he
uttered one night, to one of his faithful friends,
this phrase, which sounds like a knell, " Look !
my flesh is ripening for the tomb."

I return to my story.   The old *emigré*
marquis, Armand, not choosing to leave the
bones of a Villiers de l'Isle Adam in England,
returned to France towards 1820, and died,
soon after the birth of the poet, in a little
manor-house, whose only tower overlooks the
port of Légué and the tossing expanse of the
Bay of St. Brieuc.   He left four children,
two sons and two daughters.   One, Gabrielle,

became a nun, and died not long ago, a sister
of the Sacré Cœur de' Jésus. The other
married, when no longer young, a Mons. du
Rumain. This worthy couple never showed
any great tenderness for their nephew, either
during his life or after his death. The
youngest brother, Victor, entered the priest-
hood very early in life. He was a wise and
saintly man. He refused all honours, and
would never leave the poor parish of Ploumilliau, of which he was for half a century
the devoted rector. His nephew has dedicated to him one of the most extraordinary
of his tales, "L'Intersigne." It was written
in 1875 in the presbytery of the good and
simple priest; and the sojourn of the great
and unhappy poet (whose life at that time
was all storm, agitation, and care) in the
peace of that quiet retreat, inspired him with
these wonderful lines, which none who knew
and loved him can read without emotion :

"The rural aspect of this house, with its
green-shuttered windows, its three stone steps,
its tangle of ivy, clematis, and tea-roses,
covering the walls and reaching the roof

(whence a little cloud of smoke escaped through a chimney topped by a vane), inspired me with a feeling of calm, of well-being, of profound peace. The trees of a neighbouring orchard showed through the trellised enclosure, their leaves all rusted by the exhausting summer heats. The two windows of the only storey shone with the western fire. Between them was a hollow niche holding the image of some happy saint. Silently I dismounted, fastening my horse to the window-shutter, and as I raised the knocker I cast a traveller's glance at the horizon behind me. But so brightly did that horizon shine over the wild and distant forests of oak and pine, whither the last birds were winging their belated way, so solemnly did the waters of a distant reed-covered lake reflect the sky, so beautiful was nature in the calm air of that deserted spot, at that moment when the silence falls, that I stood mute, the knocker still dangling in my grasp. 'O thou!' I thought, 'who findest not the refuge of thy dreams, and to whom, after many a weary march 'neath cruel stars—so joyful at the start, so saddened now—the land of Canaan with its palm-trees and running waters comes not with the dawn. Heart made for other exile than that whose bitterness thou sharest with brothers who love thee not! Behold, here mayst thou sit thee down upon the stone of melancholy— here mayst thou dream such dreams as might haunt thee in the tomb, wouldst thou truly desire to die! Come hither, then, for here the sight of the heavens shall transport thee into oblivion!'" I cite this passage, not only because it seems to me to be exceedingly beautiful, but because it really is a psychological document—one of the very rare instances in which a writer has permitted his published work to reflect his personal emotion.

The renunciation of the world by the young sister and brother of Villiers was not perhaps altogether the result of an irresistible vocation. In these old races, the family spirit is traditional, and the sacrifice of the earthly interest of its younger members on the altar of the birthright of the eldest, is still not unfrequently made. However this may have been, the Marquis Joseph de Villiers de l'Isle Adam, Knight of the Order of Malta "de la Langue de France," remained in consequence of that fact the only representative of his mighty line. He obtained a dispensation from the Pope, and married Mdlle. Marie Françoise le Nepveu de Carfort, who was the mother of our Villiers. The Marquis de l'Isle Adam did not derogate from his dignity by allying himself with this family. The knight Roland de Carfort took the Cross in 1248. In 1370 Olivier de Carfort allied himself with the Dukes of Brittany. At the time of the first reform of the nobility in 1669, the De Carfort family proved seven generations. It appears in the registers of nobility from 1425 to 1535, for the parishes of Cesson, Le Fœil, St. Turiaff, and Plaintel, in the bishopric of St. Brieuc. The Nepvou, or Le Nepveu, were lords of Carfort, Beruen, La Roche, Crénan, Du Clos, La Cour, La Ville Anne, Lescouët, and La Coudraye. They bore as arms, "De gueules à six billettes d'argent, 3, 2, 1 au chef de même."

I ask indulgence for my long dissertation on these genealogical details. There was but one weak spot in the coat of mail woven of pride and haughty scorn with which Villiers endued himself before he descended into the terrible lists of life. The polished vipers of the boulevards, the jealous carrion-crows of literature, knew well that to poison and wound this invulnerability, their bites and their beak-thrusts must be directed against his family pride. They did not fail to do it! His right to everything was disputed, ancestors, nobility, his very name! Villiers used to roar like a lion stung by poisonous flies. But good, clear, precise proofs are worth more to the actual public than the loudest roars, and if in that country beyond the grave he still troubles concerning trivial earthly matters, he will rejoice that his Breton cousin has endeavoured to establish incontestably his relationship with those heroes of the sword from whom, himself a hero of the pen, he so worthily descended.

Unfortunately, it is possible to be at the same time exceedingly well-born and exces-

sively poor; and Mdlle. de Carfort was no
richer than the marquis. Nevertheless, thanks
to an old aunt, Mdlle. Danièle Kerinou, who
had adopted her and who possessed a modest
competence; thanks, too, to some remnants of
fortune, and to the fabulous cheapness of life
in Brittany in those days, the household
might have lived with dignity, dividing the
year between the modest residence on the
sea-coast and the little old house in the Rue
Houvenagues at St. Brieuc.   But the singular
disposition and the perilous whimsicality of
the head of the family spoilt everything.

I do not believe that there has ever existed
either in reality or in fiction a character more
extraordinary than that of the father of Villiers.
To depict it, even approximately, would need
all the raciness of Dickens, all the profound
power of observation of Balzac.   And besides,
I should be carried too far by the subject.
I will content myself, therefore, with sketching
one salient trait of this wonderfully original
man.   The Marquis de l'Isle Adam was
possessed with an effulgent dazzling vision of
gold.   His son was haunted in the same way,

and he has thus described himself in one of his novels: "My sole inheritance, alas! has consisted in his dazzling hopes and dreams! Indifferent to the political cares of the century and of the Fatherland—indifferent, too, to the temporary results of the criminal failures of their representatives—I linger to gaze upon the reddening crests of the neighbouring forest; instinctively, though why I know not, I shun the ill-omened moonlight and the noxious presence of my fellow-men. Yes, I shun them! For I feel that I bear in my soul the reflected glory of the barren wealth of many a forgotten king."

But whereas the writer found in the exercise of his art an outlet for his besetting idea, and a defence against its allurements, the marquis formed the wild project of realizing his visions by becoming a man of business. And a singular business man was he—this tall, thin marquis! Always in the clouds—full of *morgue*, and haughty as a descendant of the "Porte Oriflamme of France" might well be; gifted, truly, with an all-devouring activity, but spending it all in placing shares in the most chimerical of undertakings ! He asserted, and with some show of reason, that during the Revolution, and the troublous times that ensued, many inheritances were wrongly assigned to people who had no right to them, and this to the detriment of the real heirs. On this supposition his principal speculation depended. He undertook, in consideration of a certain percentage, to have restored to the injured families the properties which were theirs by right. This brilliant project once formed, the marquis went forth, beating up the country in every direction, searching private libraries, public archives, and church registers ; talking to old people, and accumulating a formidable mass of information. Then, when he considered himself sufficiently armed, apprizing those who were most interested. Some, seduced by the hope of gain, allowed themselves to be tempted, and after long and expensive litigation, ended by consigning the marquis and his imaginary inheritances to all the gods of Erebus. This discoverer of doubtful inheritances soon became the terror of every attorney, lawyer,

c

and sheriffs' officer in Lower Brittany. For his haughty self-confidence carried him every-where, into every office, every agency; and his cool pride, his aristocratic ways, and his illustrious name, awed the worthy scriveners of a remote province, where people are still simple enough to respect certain things. It will easily be conceived that such under-takings and the failure which generally crowned them, far from augmenting the redoubtable marquis's income, made fresh gaps in his patrimony.

And the second speculation undertaken by this astonishing person was as fantastic as the first. Dreaming, as he did incessantly, of delusive treasure, he soon began to imagine that it existed elsewhere than in his own fancy. He persuaded himself that the soil of old Armorica concealed subterranean caves, mute guardians of the fabulous riches placed in them by former generations in times of trouble and civil war.

Where, for example, was the huge fortune of the Villiers de l'Isle Adam, which had enabled them to take rank amongst the most

gorgeous courtiers of France? The seeker
of inheritances became a treasure seeker, and
set himself to work with the same ardour
and conviction as heretofore. In the neigh-
bourhood of Quintin stood the ruins of an
old castle, which had formerly belonged to the
Villiers de l'Isle Adam. The marquis bought
a concession, hired labourers, and set about
his researches. I know not whether he had
discovered in his family archives, some proof,
or even any vague indication, which might
lead to success. His son was convinced he
had. He has spoken to me very seriously
and eloquently of this treasure, buried for
centuries; he has shown me the plan of the
subterranean hiding-place, and he endeavoured
to find capitalists to assist his father in com-
pleting his excavations.

Fortunately money was not to be had, and
Villiers, not having been able to carry out
this dream in a practical way, has realized it
in a wonderful manner in one of his most
powerful works. I speak of the book entitled
" Le Vieux de la Montagne," the full and
complete manuscript of which I have held

in my hands.   This drama, according to the poet's design, should have immediately followed that of " Axël," of which it is the continuation, as " The Adoration of the Magi " is the conclusion.

CHAPTER II.

HILE her husband was thus spending himself in a feverish and ruinous activity, the gentle and delicate marquise lived sadly on at home in the company of her good aunt Kerinou. The existence of these two women was solitary and sad, the anxiety which the undertakings of the head of the family caused Mdme. de l'Isle Adam alone breaking its monotony; but a fervent piety, a rare gentleness of soul, and a strong hope in the goodness of God, supported her through life. Her faith was at last rewarded, and God granted her most ardent desire, by sending her in November, 1838, a son who was the joy, the belief, the hope, and the pride of her simple existence. Never did a great artist have a more admirable mother! During her long life she never wavered once in her faith in him, and in his genius. She believed in her son with the same simple trust with which she believed in her God.

It is easy to conceive with what joy the advent of this child was hailed by these two lonely women. Here was a being to love, to cherish, to bring up—sunshine breaking in upon the monotony of their darkness. The marquis, too, was radiant as he gazed on this offshoot of the Villiers de l'Isle Adam. Here was someone who would restore the glory of the old race. Ah! he would endow his son with fabulous wealth. He would force the earth to render up the treasure hidden in its breast! Back he went to his excavations, the marquise and her aunt seeing him depart this time with less regret, for hope and consolation smiled on the two good women from the baby's cradle.

The Bishop of St. Brieuc stood godfather to the new-comer, and baptized him, 28th November, 1838, in the presence of his grandfather, his father, and Mdlle. de Kerinou. The venerable prelate bestowed on his godson his own Christian name of Matthias.

I have no intention of following step by step the progress of the childhood of Villiers ; the most talented biographers of famous men have seldom succeeded in making the early years of their heroes interesting. For childhood is above all things a period of silent incubation, during which soul and mind are secretly and laboriously developed. One incident of these first years spent at St. Brieuc must, however, be reported, for later the imagination of Villiers embroidered it with fantastic details. He was about seven years old, when his nurse lost him out walking. A band of strolling mountebanks, who were going to Brest, met the strayed child, and looking on the sprightly fair-haired boy as their legitimate prize, laid hands on him. Some days later his father found him at Brest in the booth of his strolling captors. He was

already the pet of the company, and there
appeared to be such a bond of affection
between the chief of the poor rope-dancers
and the boy, that the marquis, overjoyed to
get back his son, relinquished all idea of prosecution.   Those who were acquainted with
Villiers will easily imagine what wonderful
and humorous tales he would weave out of
such an adventure.   It was worth listening
to, when, in picturesque style, he would con-
jure up the memories of the *two years* he had
spent amongst those admirable, though ill-
favoured gipsies, visiting successively Italy,
Germany, the Tyrol, and chivalrous Hungary
—rescued and restored at last to his family
through the devotion of a beautiful Romany
lass, the last descendant of a time-honoured
race, etc., etc.   Villiers began his education
at the school of St. Brieuc, but soon after-
wards continued it at the Lycée at Laval.
There his genius began to trouble his soul.
The divine visions of poetry hovered round
him, the breath of artistic enthusiasm fell
glowing on his brow, and his first verses were
written.   Between whiles he concluded his

classical studies, which, once finished, his
family settled with him at Rennes, in a house
in the Rue de Corbin.   At this time Villiers
de l'Isle Adam was seventeen years old, and
it was sufficient to see him for a few moments
to be convinced of his vocation.   Inspiration
beamed on his full pale forehead, it sparkled
in his discourse, in which the tumult of ideas
pressed disorderly one on the other, trembled
on his full lips already curled with irony, and
filled his clear blue eyes with a disturbing
light.   His large, fair, dishevelled head, his
strange gestures, his disorderly style of dress,
alarmed the correct provincial society, of
which, by the way, he saw but little.   But
those few privileged mortals who entered the
magic circle of his intimacy, remained there
fascinated and dazzled.   Villiers already possessed that extraordinary magnetic power
which he preserved all his life, and of which
every friend of his has felt the influence.   The
depth of thought in one so young was almost
uncanny.   All in fact he needed, at the time
of his arrival at Rennes, to fit him to pronounce his vows before the altar of art, was

that his heart should bleed under the divine wound of love, the agonizing consecration of every true poet.

It was amongst the green fields and lanes of Brittany that there arose for him, to vanish almost immediately in death, that tender vision of womanhood which was his fleeting, but his only earthly love. She was one of those entrancing creatures, of whom he has so well said, "There are certain helpmates who ennoble every one of life's joys, certain radiant maidens whose love is only positively given once. Yes, some few saintly souls, ideal in their dawning beauty." I will not profane the sacred passion of these two young hearts by trying to describe it. I will only say, They loved, and she died. On a sudden, suffering unfolded and spread the poet's budding wings. In an artist's youth, all his feelings, even sorrow, turn to song, and so it was with Villiers. These lines, written at seventeen years of age by the disdainful scoffer our generation knew so well, have their natural place here, marking, as they do, the close of the child's and the birth of the artist's existence.

I.

O charmants églantiers ! soleil, rayon, verdure !
Frais salut que la terre offre dans un murmure
De zéphirs renaissants, aux cœurs emplis d'espoir,
Bocage encor tout plein de chastes rêveries,
Six mois se sont passés loin de vos fleurs chéries :
     J'avais besoin de vous revoir.

Oh ! vous souvenez-vous, forêt délicieuse,
De la jolie enfant qui passait gracieuse,
Souriant simplement au ciel, à l'avenir,
Se perdant avec moi dans ces vertes allées ?
Eh bien ! parmi les lis de vos sombres vallées,
     Vous ne la verrez plus venir.

O printemps ! ô lilas ! ô profondes ramées !
Comme autrefois vos fleurs, qu'elle avait tant aimées,
Sous vos sentiers déserts exhalent leurs amours ;
L'aubépine s'enlace au banc de la charmille,
L'oiseau chante, le ciel est bleu, le soleil brille :
     Rien n'a changé dans les beaux jours !

Silencieux vallon ! cela n'était qu'un rêve,
Un songe radieux qui maintenant s'achève
Et ne laisse après lui qu'un amer souvenir . . .
Ne me demandez pas ce qu'elle est devenue,
La pauvre jeune fille en ce monde venue
     Pour consoler et pour mourir !

Morte ! et je suis encore en proie à l'existence !
C'est donc cela la vie ? Et déjà mon enfance
A-t-elle disparu loin de ce cœur brisé ?

Seigneur, vous êtes grand, mais vous êtes sévère !
Ainsi me voilà seul : c'est fini sur la terre ;
    Cela s'appelle : " le Passé."

II.

Hélas ! je me souviens.   Les vents au sein des ombres,
Du fleuve harmonieux plissaient les vagues sombres ;
Les chants ailés du soir s'étaient évanouis ;
Et la lune, en glissant parmi les blancs nuages,
Souvent illuminait les teintes des feuillages
    Du clair obscur des belles nuits.

Le rossignol, caché sous l'épaisse feuillée,
Modulait les soupirs de sa chanson perlée,
Les fleurs, dans leurs parfums, s'endormaient à leur tour ;
Et comme deux rayons réunissent leur flamme,
Tous deux nous unissions nos âmes dans une âme,
    Et nos deux cœurs dans notre amour.

Comme son joli pied se posait sur la mousse !
Comme sa chevelure était soyeuse et douce !
Nous allions, enlacés, sous les hauts peupliers ;
Elle avait dix-sept ans ; j'avais cet âge à peine,
Souvent le rossignol retenait son haleine
    En écoutant nos pas légers.

Et moi je contemplais mon amante pensive,
Et nous nous en allions, seuls, auprès de la rive.
Sa main sur mon épaule et le front sur ma main ;
Et les frémissements de la nuit solitaire
Emportaient dans les cieux, ainsi qu'une prière,
    Tous les doux songes du chemin.

III.

Puis, le réveil ! la mort ! l'existence qui change !
O temps ! vieillard glacé ! qu'as-tu fait de mon ange ?
Où l'as-tu mise, hélas ! et froide et pour toujours ?
Qu'as-tu fait de l'enfant jeune et pleine de charmes,
Qu'as-tu fait du sourire et qu'as-tu fait des larmes,
        Oh ! qu'as-tu fait de nos amours ?

IV.

Voyez comme les fleurs viennent bien près des tombes !
On dirait un bouquet que les jeunes colombes,
Retournant au pays, nous laissent pour adieu.
—Qu'avait-elle donc fait pour mourir la première ?
Est-ce un crime de vivre ? et l'amour, sur la terre,
        N'est-il pas le pardon de Dieu ?

Ne me souriez plus, ô campagne immortelle !
Je suis seul maintenant ; si ce n'était pour elle,
Je n'avais pas besoin de vos fraîches beautés ;
N'ai-je pas vu l'abîme où tombent toutes choses ?
Les lis meurent dans l'ombre où se fanent les roses :
        Les cyprès seuls restent plantés.

Elle est sous les cyprès, la pâle jeune femme !
Mon amour triste et fier brûle encor dans mon âme,
Comme une lampe d'or veille sur le cercueil.
Mais je ne pleure plus : la douleur a ses charmes.
Et d'ailleurs, ô mon Dieu, mes yeux n'ont plus de larmes,
        Et mon cœur seul porte le deuil.

I.

O lovely eglantine ! O sunlit glades !
Fresh greeting offered by the murmuring earth
On circling breezes to all hopeful hearts,
Since last I saw those fair and much-loved flowers,
Which yet fill all your memory-haunted groves,
Six weary months have passed,
      And I have longed to look on you again !

Dost thou remember, Forest, lovely yet,
The pretty graceful child who wandered by,
Smiling her simple faith in Heaven and Fate,
And straying with me through your verdant maze ?—
Alas ! the lilies hidden in your green depths
      Shall see her pass no more !

O spring-time ! Lilacs ! O deep greenwood shades !
Your flowers, erstwhile so dear to her sweet soul,
Still shed their scent o'er your deserted paths,
The may still twines the bench within the grove,
Birds sing, the sky is blue, the sun still shines,
      No change has come upon your summer-tide !

Dumb silent valley ! It was all a dream,
A radiant dream, too soon, alas ! to pass—
And leaving but a bitter sense of loss—
Where she is now, I pray you, ask me not !
That sweet young creature, sent into this world
      To comfort others—then herself to die !

Dead ! Can it be ? And I must still live on !
Is this Life's fate ? And has my youth indeed
Forsaken for ever this poor broken heart ?

Lord, Thou art just, but oh ! Thou strikest hard !
I am alone ! I've done with earthly dreams !
    I've learnt the bitter meaning of "The Past !"

II.

Alas ! I see it still ! Out of the shadowy night
The gentle river flowed in darkly rippling waves ;
Fallen into dreamless sleep, the birds had hushed their
        songs,
The moonbeams creeping slow athwart the fleecy clouds
Touched with their silver light the dusk and massy shades,
    Seen through the twilight of the lovely night.

The nightingale from out the green and bosky shade
Sighed forth his passion in his pearly-throated song,
The flowers had bowed their heads in deep and perfumed
        sleep,
And we, whose souls were joined as though in one sun ray,
    Could feel our happy hearts beating in one great
        love !

How firm her dainty step upon the mossy path !
How silken and how soft the masses of her hair !
As arm in arm we walked 'neath the tall poplar trees,
(She was but seventeen, and I was hardly more,)
Often the nightingale would seem to hold his breath,
    To listen to our lightly falling steps.

And how I loved to gaze upon her thoughtful face,
As far along the bank we wandered all alone,
My shoulder 'neath her hand, while mine caressed her
        brow,

And all the rustlings of the lovely night
Carried to Heaven, as though they were a prayer,
    The sweet and dreamy fancies of the hour !

III.

Then, with Death's awful change, the sad awakening
    came !
O hoary-headed Time ! Where hast thou hid my love ?
For ever cold and still, ah ! whither is she gone ?
That child, so full of life, of young resistless charm,
Where is her magic smile ? and where her melting tears ?
    And where the vanished glory of our loves ?

IV.

Mark now, how lush the flowers grow near a tomb !
Just like the nosegays some young turtle doves
Might leave for farewell offering, ere they fly
Into their native country ! Why should she die first ?
Is life a crime ? And is not earthly love
    God's own forgiveness ?

Smile then no more, O immortal country fields !
I stand henceforth alone.   And it was but for her
That your fresh blooming beauty seemed so sweet to me !
Have I not plumbed the depths which ingulf all earthly
    hope ?
The lilies wither, and the roses fade away
    Beneath the shadows which the cypress loves !

Beneath the cypress sleeps that woman young and pale,
My sad and faithful love still burns within my soul,

Like to the golden lamp which burns before a corpse.
But I can weep no more, in spite of sorrow's charm,
And this, O Lord, is why : My eyes have no more
    tears,
  And my heart hides its lonely misery !

Villiers never loved truly, deeply, ingenuously, but this once. No other woman ever took in his existence the place of the gentle, dead Breton girl. His imagination may have been swept away by the rustle of some passing robe, his senses may have been captivated, his artistic feeling interested, by the charm of the perturbing mystery which surrounds the eternal problem of the softer sex, but the poet's heart remained untouched, impregnable, proud, wrapped up in its sad fidelity to that early memory.

This first terrible experience of sorrow hastened the prodigiously rapid intellectual development of the young writer. He sought and found refuge in excessive activity, and Inspiration, great and radiant consoler, illumined his mind and beamed upon his heart. Vast conceptions, gigantic projects, such as are always formed by youthful artists, enveloped his spirit with their luxuriant growth. In this one year, he conceives the idea of a drama, " Morgane," impressed with a melancholy splendour ; he plans a wonderful trilogy, which eventually, under the three titles of " Axël," " L'Adoration des Mages," and " Le Vieux de la Montagne," will become the chief work, the crowning point of his existence as a thinker ; he imagines his mysterious novel, " Isis," and, above all, he pours forth in lines pulsating with life and glow, all the tumultuous grief of his tortured and sorrow-laden soul !

During this period, while his genius was agitatedly beating her wings like a captive eagle, Villiers de l'Isle Adam found at the home-fireside constant encouragement, unceasing sympathy, and immeasurable tenderness ! There is something admirably touching and rare in this worship of him by his own people in his early days.   Generally the youth of an artist is darkened by the ill-will, the instinctive mistrust of art, the narrow-mindedness, the love of lucre, of his family.   In the case of Villiers de l'Isle Adam, the contrary was the fact.   The mother, the old aunt, the treasure-seeking marquis, disagreeing in all else, formed a perfect union when it was a question of singing the praises of "their Matthias." They lauded him, they exalted him on to a pedestal. His vocation, his genius, the certainty of his success, of his future glory, were so many articles of faith to them. And they proved it.

Persuaded that Paris was the only stage worthy of the great part which their Matthias was called to enact, convinced that it was their own absolute duty to sacrifice everything in order that the genius of the family might expand in full freedom, these admirable souls, at the very sight of whom the self-important bourgeois smiled and shrugged their shoulders, resolved to sell everything, to realize their little fortune, and, their small purse in hand, to go and await in some out-of-the-way corner in the formidable town the final victory of the last of the Villiers de l'Isle Adam, who, according to their childlike faith, was with brain and pen to reconquer for them the fortune and the celebrity which their ancestors had won by blood and sword !

All hastened to the rescue. The nun of the Sacred Heart, the abbé, the old aunt—the marquis was indefatigable in calling in his funds; he sold at an enormous loss, but without a shadow of regret, his little manor-house at Légué and the old residence at St. Brieuc. He abandoned the excavations for ten treasures, and the search for half a hundred inheritances, and following his son, accompanied by his wife, and having in tow the old aunt, who would not be left behind, he started for Paris, to the cry of "Dieu le volt!" (It is God's will!) with the same confidence in which his crusader ancestors had departed to Jerusalem.

CHAPTER III.

AT the time of the exodus of Villiers
and his family, Paris had become,
from the artistic and literary point
of view, the paradise of the common-place. The gods of this Olympus were
composers of operettas, manufacturers of
serial novels, historiographers of the latest
scandals, poets of the drawing-room, of the

boudoir, nay, of the café concerts. All these
lived and fattened on their trade, honoured,
and almost celebrated, clinging to the title of
artist, yet ignorant of, or despising, the pri-
mordial rules of art. The censure, which
smiled sanctimoniously on the short skirts
and sprightly whims of the Offenbach School,
could never be severe enough on truly artistic
and conscientious work. It was the epoch of
the ridiculous prosecution of the author of
" Madame Bovary," and of the sentence
against Baudelaire.

As for those poets who pursued their
divine chimera with fervour and disinterestedness, no jest was reckoned too coarse, no insult
in too bad taste, to be thrown in their faces.
The press was perpetually sharpening the
arrows of its keenest satire, wherewith to
pierce whomsoever aspired to any great ideal.
Victor Hugo, exiled as he was, alone succeeded in stirring the masses to their depths.
In the face of all this opprobrium, the last
survivors of the admirable phalanx of romantic
poets had wrapped themselves in scornful
silence. Emile Deschamps lay dying ob-

scurely in the dreary town of Versailles, he, the author of the " Romanceros," rhyming sickly madrigals to Chloris ; while the divine Théophile Gautier, the illustrious hero of the first performance of " Hernani," cast the last blossoms of his astonishing intellect on the common track of the newspaper feuilleton. Poetry and art seemed in truth to be dead, stifled by the triumph of materialistic stupidity. But poetry and art are as immortal as the starry heavens, and at the very moment in which they seemed to lie in their last agony, they were silently making ready to spread their vigorous limbs and soar with lofty flight into the blue realms of the ideal !

Certain youths, very young and poor, banded together in the same faith, the same deep and passionate love of the beautiful, the same lively hatred of the common-place and the vulgar, formed the bold project of revolting, weak and almost defenceless as they were, against this formidable tyranny of folly and mediocrity. They resolved to defend the sacred domain of literature with all their young strength against the invasion which

threatened it ; to proclaim the power of
rhythm, the respect that is due to syntax, to
affirm, in short, that no work can be really
artistic without a constant jealousy for form.
The critics of the chief newspapers, the
chroniclers of the small ones, drew upon their
usual arsenal of gibes and jeers, and old jokes
turned out as new, to scoff down these rash
youths.　They were given strange nicknames,
" Formists," "Stylists," " Fantaisistes," " Im-
passibles."　Songs were made about them,
they were caricatured, made to play the parts
of idiots in the " Revues" at the end of each
year, and to conclude, when a young publisher, who (thanks to his lucky daring) had
become a millionaire, ventured to publish the
first number of their collected poems, " Le
Parnasse Contemporain," they were held up
to public laughter and indignation as " Les
Parnassiens " (the Parnassians).

All this rage, however, far from crushing
these chivalrous young votaries of the ideal,
filled their hearts with fresh courage.　In spite
of jests and insults, they pursued their course,
and what is still more admirable and touching,

pursued it in spite of the direst poverty.   Of
them, as of every artist, posterity has been
the true judge; and it has sent back to their
native obscurity those who, from the heights
of their brilliant existence, made game of the
poor little feverish-eyed, shabby-coated poets.
Where are now the names of those sparkling
and witty quill-drivers, who poured forth their
sarcasms on the obscure Parnassians?   And,
on the other hand, the names of these same
Parnassians, are they not now familiar to us
all?   To cite only the chief among them, have
we not François Coppée, Sully Prudhomme,
Alphonse Daudet, Léon Cladel, Glatigny,
Catulle Mendès, and Villiers de l'Isle Adam?

Res miranda! The first publication of these
new representatives of "la jeune France"
was not a collection of verses, it was just
simply a review in which prose and poetry
joyously alternated.   Gaily covered, cheerful
in tone, with an attractive and well-sounding
title, its editor was nineteen years old, and it
had not a contributor who counted more than
five-and-twenty summers.   In short, it was
the "Revue Fantaisiste," whose director was

a native of Bordeaux, newly arrived in Paris, poor as Job and handsome as Apollo, by name Catulle Mendès. The offices of this review were in the Passage Mirès, now Passage des Princes. Here Villiers de l'Isle Adam broke his first lance, and my readers will doubtless appreciate this quotation from a little known but amusing work, in which the former director of the " Revue Fantaisiste " has presented, in a style at once witty and feeling, the picture of the home of the " Parnasse Contemporain " :—

" The office was a somewhat strange-looking place; hangings of green and rose-coloured chintz, like a smiling meadow, seemed to gaze in wonder at the mahogany cupboards and tables. A lounge (seldom unoccupied) at the back of the room appeared to sulk at the leathern arm-chair and the cardboard manuscript cases. It was half drawing-room, and would fain have been all boudoir!

" Hither, every afternoon, towards three o'clock, came Théodore de Banville, giving us freely, with the good-nature of a youthful *maestro*, his intoxicating mixture of Orpheus

and Balzac, at one and the same time so lyric
and so truly Parisian; Charles Asselineau,
with his long soft hair already grey, and on
his lips that smile, tender though ironic, which
none but Nodier ever had before him; Léon
Golzan, who graciously vouchsafed us the
support of his name; Charles Monselet,
Jules Noriac, Philoxène Boyer, dreaming of
Shakespeare, and Charles Baudelaire, slight,
elegant, a little stealthy, almost alarming with
his half-frightened air, gracefully haughty,
with the attraction and charm of beauty in
distress, rather like a very delicate bishop,
somewhat fallen away from grace perhaps,
who had donned an elaborate lay costume for
travelling purposes: ' His Eminence Mon-
seignor Beau Brummel ! ' He used to bring
us those wonderful prose poems, which are
numbered now amongst the most perfect
pages in French literature. There, too, Albert
Glatigny, with his vagrant flow of speech,
hand on hip, his necktie undone, his waistcoat
too short, and obstinately ignorant of braces,
smiling like some young faun, wearied out by
the tendernesses of the nymphs, would recite

to us those amorous strophes of his, whose rhymes seem to re-echo the sound of kisses."

It was in this abode, with its strange charm, where the three twin sisters, Youth, Poetry, and Poverty, seemed to have met together, that Villiers de l'Isle Adam made his entry into the world of letters. He presented himself, almost immediately on his arrival in Paris, his pockets stuffed with his family parchments and his own manuscript compositions. At the very outset he took the office by storm, and he soon became one of the chief editors of the " Revue Fantaisiste." The brilliant apparition of the last descendant of the Grand Master of the Knights of Malta has often been described in enthusiastic terms by those who were eye-witnesses of it. " He impressed us," says M. Henri Laujol, "as being the most magnificently gifted young man of his generation." Villiers brought with him some manuscript poems, which were published that very year by Scheuring of Lyons, with much luxury of paper and printing, under the title of " Premières Poésies " (First Poems). The book was dedicated to the Comte Alfred

de Vigny.   In this collection of verse, now
hardly to be found, there is already a glimpse
of the profound original thinker, scornful of
all conventionalism.   It is not, to be sure, by
any means a piece of perfection, but through
its uncertainties, its weaknesses, its gropings
in the dark, here and there, as in " Hermosa "
and " Le Chant du Calvaire," there beams
the flash of genius.

These first years of Villiers in Paris contain the few truly happy moments of a life
full of bitterness.   He was free, then, from
the anxiety of earning his daily bread, and
when he left the family circle, where he was
adored like a deity, he met everywhere, on
his first appearance, with an enthusiastic welcome.   The originality of his gestures and
demeanour, and his profound, passionate, and
picturesque speech, full as it was of glowing
imagery, aroused amongst young people an
admiration which amounted to fanaticism.
He was the spoiled child of the Parnassians,
and he found in their *coterie* the two friends
who, through all the trials and hardships, and
all the mortifications of his life, remained

faithful to him till death, and after it; I
speak of M. Stéphane Mallarmé and M.
Léon Dierx.   Every friend of Villiers must,
like myself, vow an infinite gratitude to
the two excellent-hearted poets who, having
supported the author of the " Nouveau
Monde " in the hours of his despondency and
darkest poverty, showed him, in his last illness, a care, a delicate tenderness, a devotion,
and a disinterestedness, which the tenderest
woman might have envied them.   No artist's
existence, even in the direst tribulation, could
be completely wretched, while brightened and
warmed by the flame of such sturdy friendship.

Villiers de l'Isle Adam made his *début*,
then, in the " Revue Fantaisiste," with a tale
called " Claire Lenoir," a strange, mysterious,
terrifying story.   What makes this work
peculiarly interesting to us is that in it there
appears, for the first time, a character which
has become almost legendary, and on the
creation of which the writer worked up till
the end of his life.   It will be understood
that I refer to the striking figure of Dr.
Triboulat Bonhomet, the personification of

the scientific and atheistic bourgeois—a
monstrous Prud'homme, transcendently foolish and ferociously egotistic.   In drawing his
own portrait, Bonhomet writes this sentence,
which seems to me to sum up the original
idea of his author : " My physiognomy is that
of my century, of which I have reason to
believe myself the archetype ; briefly, I am a
doctor, a philanthropist, and a man of the
world."   Again, speaking of his own convictions, he says : " My religious ideas are
limited to the absurd conviction that God has
created man in His own image, and *vice versâ*."
This Dr. Triboulat Bonhomet was to Villiers
what "le garçon" was to Flaubert : a sort of
imaginary personage, whom he endued with a
complete personality, with all the passions of
a real and complicated character, in whose
mouth he placed the jokes and the aphorisms
which he collected in conversation and in life,
or which his profound and ironic wit invented
for him.   This doctor makes one shudder rather
than laugh, and the circumstantial pedantry
with which he relates the alarming adventures
of "that discreet and scientific personage,

Dame Claire Lenoir, widow," adds to the terror of her story.

But I shall frequently have occasion, in the course of these notes, to quote the sayings of this "honorary member of many academies and professor of physiology," whose greatest enjoyment, according to his biographer, was to kill swans, in order to hear their dying song. For the moment, I must register the decease of the poetical little review, in which so many talents tried their budding wings. It passed away in the second year of its existence, beaten to death by the censure, in the name of public morality. The so-called outrage had been committed by its director, Catulle Mendès, and took the form of a one-act comedy in verse, entitled, "A Night's Romance" ("Le Roman d'une Nuit"). The piece was far from being a good one, but, though frivolous and mediocre, it was not criminal, and one wonders on reading it how judges were found to condemn the author of such a tiny spark to a month's imprisonment, and the review which published it to 500 francs fine. The poet had to go to Ste.

Pélagie and the review had to pay the fine.
Money was scarce, and by the time the
demands of justice were satisfied, the cashbox
was empty. The contributors cheerfully celebrated the obsequies of their literary offspring,
and most of them went to live in a furnished
inn in the Rue Dauphine, famous in the annals
of contemporary literature as the Blue Dragon
Hotel. Four years later, we find them
gathered once more round their former chief.
Fortune had smiled on Catulle Mendès; he had
money in his pockets, and owned, in the Rue
de Douai, an apartment containing real furniture and a piano ; likewise a groom, surnamed
Covielle, who opened the door to such visitors
as were in possession of the necessary pass-
word. In one of his articles in the " Patrie,"
these meetings of the future Parnassians have
been admirably reproduced by François Coppée. Want of space forbids me to cite the
whole, but I quote this portrait of Villiers de
l'Isle Adam, which represents him with perfect
and striking truthfulness.

"Suddenly, round the assembled poets, runs
the universal cry of joy, ' Villiers ! Here's

Villiers !' And all at once a young man, with light blue eyes, a little wavering in his walk, chewing a cigarette, tossing back his disordered locks, and twisting his small, fair moustache, enters, wearing a haggard look, shakes hands absently, sees the open piano, sits down to it, and nervously touching the keys, sings in a voice which trembles, but the deep and magic accents of which none of us can ever forget, a melody he has improvised in the street, a vague, mysterious *melopœia*, which accompanies (thereby doubling the depth and agitation of the impression it makes) Charles Baudelaire's beautiful sonnet:

'Nous aurons des lits pleins d'odeurs légères
Des divans profonds comme des tombeaux,' etc.

'Our beds shall be scented with sweetest perfume,
Our divans be as cool and as dark as the tomb!'

"Then, while all are still under the spell, humming the last notes of his air, or else abruptly breaking it off, he rises, leaves the piano, goes as though to hide himself in the corner of the room, and rolling another cigarette, casts over his stupified audience a comprehensive glance, the glance of Hamlet as he lies at Ophelia's feet, during the representation of the death of Gonzago.

" Thus appeared to us, eighteen years ago, in those pleasant gatherings at the house of Catulle Mendès, in the Rue de Douai, the Comte Auguste Philippe Villiers de l'Isle Adam."—*Patrie*, Feb. 26, 1883.

CHAPTER IV.

IT sometimes happens that strong
influences felt by an artist in his
early intellectual life leave an in-
effaceable mark on his existence.
At the time of his initiation into literature,
Villiers fell under two such influences, that
of Charles Baudelaire, and that of my father.

The ascendancy exercised over him by the "Satanic" poet seems to me to have been somewhat inauspicious. It developed his taste for extremes and for mystification, it led him astray from the exercise of his talent, naturally clear and simple in its expression, instigating him to bury it in clouds of whimsical metaphor, or to allow himself to be drawn into the obscurities, the affectations, the over-refinements, which sometimes disfigure his work, and make it so difficult to read. Let it be understood that I do not speak here of irony, which was one of Villiers' most powerful weapons, and which was originally, in his case, thoroughly good-natured, though the hardships of life, and the wicked stupidity of those who considered themselves "the pink of gentility," sharpened it, and rendered it pitiless and terrible.

But his connection with Baudelaire, the influence which the author of the "Fleurs du Mal" gained over his heart and intellect at the threshold of his literary career, inspired him with that mania for making the middle class stare, "épater le bourgeois," and for mystifying his readers, from which he was never able to free himself even in his most deeply thought-out work, " L'Eve Future."

My father's influence, on the contrary, was, by Villiers' own acknowledgment, very useful and precious to him. He often told me that he would have risen much higher if he had listened to him more. But there was nothing strange in the fact that his nervous nature, his mind full of every sort of curiosity, his youth, indeed, should have been much more captivated by the wilful eccentricities, the exotic life, the dandyism, and the cool perversity of Charles Baudelaire, than by the counsels of his Breton relative, who was for ever preaching to him sobriety, labour, solitude, and silence.

Up to the time of the arrival of the family of Villiers de l'Isle Adam in Paris, my father's relations with Villiers had merely been those which usually exist between a youth and a man considerably his senior; but, after the young poet's triumphant entry into the capital, attracted more than any other person by the brilliant dawn of the budding genius, and dreading for him the formidable reefs on which so many great men make shipwreck during their apprentice days, he drew Villiers towards him, and took him, so to say, under his wholesome tutorship. From that day, Matthias became part of the family, and it was soon after that he paid that first visit to Fougères my recollection of which I have described at the commencement of this work.

Here, perhaps, is the fittest place to insert an amusing letter, the facsimile of which is offered to the inquiring reader. It is addressed to my father, and dated from Montfort, a small town in the department of Ille-et-Vilaine.   In it Villiers alludes to the printing of his first volume of poems. M. Lemenant, the lawyer-friend in whose house the letter was written, was a worthy and eccentric man, an old schoolfellow of the poet's at Laval, who, having profited but little by his earlier education at school, and by his subsequent study of transcendental philosophy in Paris, wisely devoted himself to the care of the parental acres and briefs, in his native province.   He died young and rich. Villiers dedicated some verses to him in the " Premières Poésies."

" My dear good poet,

"And how are you ? Better I hope. If I were in your place, I should be in the rudest health. But let that be as it may, I am certain that the one thing that you pine for at this moment, is your seventy-second game of chess.

"If, however, you should be thinking of starting for the land of shadows, be good enough to give me warning, so that I may compose in your glory, and for the wonderment of the world in general, a funeral march in E flat. It is the fashionable key, and on fashion I take my stand !

"I have no letters from my interesting family. Lemenant and I are in the depths of poverty, which fact forces me to ask your permission to put off the repayment of your kindly help. Don't swear at me ! I publish the praise of your amiability far and wide. And, besides, the fault is yours, and it will teach you to be too good-natured ! Now, I ask you, whether in this nineteenth century, any sane man should lend money to his friend? Do you desire to see the finger of scorn pointed at you in every drawing-room you enter? I will denounce you to the whole of society as a traitor to the principle of modern selfishness!

"This may bore you—but you richly deserve it!

"The proofs of 'Master Perrin' are comical to the last degree.

"Lemenant and I have had several hearty laughs at his expense. I am going to write him a little jeering letter which will puzzle his poor brains.

"Here is a specimen of his manner. It is all the same from beginning to end.

"'*L'uſaige de Don Ivan & deſ pêchevrſ dv golfe.*'

"'L'usage de Don Juan et des pêcheurs du golfe.'

"Here you have an impossible rhyme, printed in this man's extraordinary style. Too much of a joke, isn't it? Between ourselves, a man who has such a notion must be mad; just fancy a book printed on yellow paper in this style! Lemenant vows it would be quite phosphorescent. It really is comical, and in my collected works (if they are ever published) I might afford myself such a luxury, but at present! *Zut!* This is my definition. He is the *ne plus ultra* of a grinning, superannuated typographer, or, if you prefer it, the weird ink-scratcher of the Gutenbergian Press! and, in other words, the grave of human thought!

"Now, let us go on to less casual matters.

"Montfort is a town, or rather—stay! I am right in calling it a town—full of mud, and of calm.—We live in it, under the wing of that good old seraph whose name is 'cheerfulness.'

"The country swarms with worthy people, and one hardly knows oneself, coming from Paris!

"There is a mill here, a real mill, exactly like Rosa Bonheur's pictures (still life).

"Lemenant pours daily from our open window his sanctimonious speeches, and his metaphysico-transcendental spleen.

" The few terrified passers-by listen, listen, —and accompany his discourse to the air, 'Il a des bott, bott, bott.' The which produces an effect whereon I heartily congratulate him.

"We live in the square, which triples the interest of the view, and I peacefully go on making rhymes in the midst of the tumult. *A bientôt*, dear kind poet!

" Believe in my true faithful friendship! I clasp your hand and heartily embrace you. If you have time, send me a reassuring word about your health.

" VILLIERS DE L'ISLE ADAM."

At the very end of the Rue Richelieu, almost opposite the Théâtre Français, stands an hotel—the Hôtel d'Orléans—where I often and gladly stay. I cannot pass under its vaulted entrance without being deeply moved. As I gaze on the inner court with its steep flight of steps, and glance at the second-floor windows, all the ghosts of my youthful school-days rise up around me, every corner of the dwelling is familiar, and at each

turn I seem to see the proud outline of my
father's face.   Here he lived for twelve years,
and here my brothers and I, students at the
Collège Rollin, spent our Sunday holidays.
We used to be present in clouds of tobacco
smoke, at endless discussions between Villiers
de l'Isle Adam and the master of the little
apartment.   We did not understand much,
it must be admitted, but we used to gaze
open-mouthed at the wild gestures, the
chamois-like bounds, the contortions of every
feature, with which our cousin Matthias used
to embellish his arguments.

This hotel in the Rue Richelieu had not
then, it has not now, the commonplace aspect
of our modern caravanserais.   In spite of
all the alterations made by its new owners,
the walls of the building still bear the marks
of its illustrious origin.

For this was the old town-house of the
Cardinal Armand de Richelieu, and the principal building, reached by a flight of stone
steps of great dignity of form, has preserved
all the majestic simplicity of the architectural
style of the time of Louis XIII.

In the days of my father and of Villiers, the hotel was kept by a worthy couple whose son was an artist, and hence, scattered through the rooms, were tapestries, frescoes, pictures, and trophies of arms, which heightened the quaint air of the dwelling.

Hither, in the evenings, to a modest apartment on the second floor, came some dreamers, some thinkers, some philosophers. Besides the face of Villiers, a second countenance, seen by chance at one of these reunions, remains graven on my memory, that of Léon Cladel. His mighty stature, his long hair, his pallid complexion, his gloomy countenance, his wild eyes, his reddish-brown beard, really gave him that air attributed to him by Catulle Mendès, of a fallen angel.

He used to come with his friend Baudelaire, whom, I am ashamed to say, I do not recollect.

As my father was much occupied with philosophy at this period of his life, the philosophers were the most numerous and eager guests at these gatherings, where much coffee was drunk, and an incalculable number of pipes and cigarettes consumed. The host was at that time passionately interested in the German school of philosophy, which soon laid hold of the profound mind of Villiers de l'Isle Adam. His friend initiated him into the brilliant spiritualist theories of Hegel, whose fervent disciple he was; but the humanitarian and socialistic projects of the author of the " Poèmes virils" found a somewhat unfriendly auditor in Villiers. His mind and soul soared too far above realities to preoccupy themselves about the sufferings of humanity or the miseries of real life. On the other hand, the Titanic poetry, the breadth and splendour of the views of the German thinker, filled him with the greatest enthusiasm. He began to put forward the theories of the speculative philosophy in the curious tale of " Claire Lenoir," which I have already spoken of. Some years later, in 1862, he published the first volume of a mysterious novel, " Isis," the continuation of which never appeared, in which the Hegelian principles and system are developed and carried out to their extremest limit.   This first volume, entitled " Tullia Fabriana," was dedicated to my father.   It gained for its author some expressions of admiration from Baudelaire, which at this date may seem excessive.

In truth, this novel contains more faults than good qualities.   The passion for romanticism of which Villiers never could rid himself, here breaks out in gloomy, improbable, melodramatic adventures, worked out with all the inexperience of a young hand.   An overflowing wealth of imagination does not suffice to conceal the inherent vices of the work.   When the writer's talent had ripened, and when time had calmed down the exuberance of his fancy, he himself recognized all the imperfections of his early efforts, and " Isis," which was originally to consist of six volumes, was not continued.   In the preface to " Tullia Fabriana " the author thus expresses himself : " 'Isis' is the title of a collection of works, which will appear, I hope, at short intervals ; it is the collective formula for a series of philosophical novels, the x of a problem of the Ideal ; it is the great unknown : once finished, the work will be its own definition."

The absolute need for oddity which seems to be inherent in Villiers, is betrayed in "Isis" in a very evident manner. The eccentricities of its style attracted many jests in the smaller papers. Already, at the appearance of "Claire Lenoir" in the "Revue Fantaisiste," the "Tintamarre" and other satirical sheets had made copious game of the strange expressions employed by the young writer. One sentence especially had become celebrated. It had been placed by the author in the lips of Dr. Bonhomet himself, " Je lui fus *grat* de cette injure." Villiers claimed that, as *ingrat* is the qualifying adjective derived from the noun *ingratitude*, so the adjective derived from *gratitude* must be *grat*. Logically, reason was on his side, but he doubtless forgot that the French language laughs at logic.

This name of Bonhomet, coming back to my pen, reminds me that this bold conception, which haunted Villiers' brain until his death, is not purely imaginary. The Hôtel d'Orléans possessed at that time, as physician in ordinary, a certain Dr. C——, who had the most ill-favoured countenance it is possible to imagine. For the rest, he was an excellent man, of a most charitable nature, and a very distinguished savant. But his gloomy face, a certain mode of expressing himself at once whimsical and pompous, his positivism, his disdainful scorn for any manifestation of art, the extraordinary shape of his hats and cut of his clothes, heated the poet's imagination. Thenceforward, all unconscious, the worthy Dr. C—— became a sort of dummy, on whose frame Villiers hung, from day to day, all the wily sophisms, all the strange fancies, all the terrible or grotesque fads, which make the savant Triboulat Bonhomet a unique type in modern literature.

The first years in Paris (1859-1863) were a most prolific period. Besides "Claire Lenoir" and "Isis," the writer gave the public two dramas full of gloomy splendour, which were never acted—"Ellen" and "Morgane." There is a fine sentence in "Morgane," which I desire to quote here, because it seems to me

F

admirably characteristic not only of the style, but of the turn of mind of Villiers de l'Isle Adam at this epoch :

"I drink to thee, O forest, thou giver of oblivion! To you, dew-laden grasses! To you, too, O wild roses! growing beneath the oaks, intoxicated by the moisture dripping from their heavy foliage! And to you, ye wild sea-shores, where hover at eventide the salt odours of the star-reflecting waves, and who stretch away, like I myself, in pride and solitude!"

The author of "L'Eve Future" always had this sense of being alone in the midst of the world. "I have always," he wrote to me a few years before his death, "felt alone, even when beside a woman I loved, or with a friend — nay, even in the enthusiastically affectionate circle of my own immediate family."

While the son thus took his place in the sunshine of literature, what became of the proud marquis, the gentle saintly marquise, the good aunt Kerinou, amidst all the noisy whirl of Parisian life? The marquis, still

possessed by his visions of wealth, had once
more taken up his lucrative speculations. He
was surrounded by a flight of birds of prey,
business agents, and such like, of strange and
lean appearance, who were engaged in sharing
amongst themselves the last remnants of his
patrimony.

He had established on his own account a
sort of branch of the Record Office, where,
with a fine, self-sufficient air, he gave out
brevets of nobility.   Unfortunately his choice
of the persons he ennobled was not always
judicious ; and thus it came about that in the
course of the trial of the poisoner, Courty de
la Pommerais, the counsel for that doctor,
criminal enough, although a homœopath, laid
before the tribunal a pompous certificate
signed by the Marquis Joseph de Villiers de
l'Isle Adam, Dean of the Order of the Knights
of Malta, and attesting the fact that the
accused, being of noble birth, had an incontestable right to bear the title of "comte"
(which title he had assumed in order to im-
pose upon his clients !).

Towards the end of 1863, somewhere about

New Year's Day, my father took me, for the first time, to visit the old Marquis and Marquise de Villiers de l'Isle Adam. They had taken apartments in the Rue St. Honoré, close to the Place Vendôme, in the house now occupied, I believe, by the photographer, M. Lejeune. I remember the drawing-room was very large, very high up, with very little furniture, and on that dark December day it made one rather shivery. The marquise appeared to me like a shadow; she was dressed in black, pale, sad, and distinguished-looking. When my father spoke of Matthias, her face beamed. She told us with a faint smile that the marquis was at his business. She added that her aunt Kerinou was ill in bed, but that she would like to see us. In a great old-fashioned bed, I perceived a little old lady, whose doll-like face, framed in an immense frilled cap, was all that could be seen of her. She had a long, mobile nose, and small bright eyes, and talked a great deal. Certain phrases which fell perpetually from her lips struck me, because they made my father laugh in spite of himself. Her intonation rests within my memory, and at this moment I can hear the little clear tremulous voice repeating, "You know, Hyacinthe, Matthias is a famous man !—Matthias is going to have a decoration.—The emperor is going to decorate Matthias.—Matthias will be decorated."

I need hardly add that it was all a dream of the old lady's. Nobody thought then, no one has thought since, of giving the "Croix" to the author of "Axël." Villiers de l'Isle Adam was one of those men whom no government decorates.

CHAPTER V.

The legend of the hoaxer hoaxed—The succession
to the throne of Greece—Villiers de l'Isle Adam a
candidate for the throne—" Le Lion de Numidie "—
" The Moor of Venice "—Nemesis—An imperial
audience—The Marquis and Baron Rothschild—
The Duc de Bassano and Villiers de l'Isle Adam—
The last act of the comedy—A poet's conclusion—
Death of Aunt Kerinou—Separation.

THERE is concerning this epoch in
the life of Villiers a wonderful
legend which has remained celebrated in the literary world; but
in passing from mouth to mouth it has gone
through so many transformations, and fallen so
far from the truth, that it is necessary to re-esta-
blish it in its pristine simplicity. My readers
will perceive that the *vis comica* of the terrible
joke of which the young writer was a victim
had no need of graces and embellishments.

Here some words of preamble are needed, and my frivolous pen must needs make an excursion into the grave and wearisome realm of contemporary political history.   Be reassured, my reader! it shall be but a short one.

In the year of grace, 1863, then, a time at which the imperial government shone with its brightest radiance, the Hellenic nation happened to be in want of a king.   The great powers who protected the heroic little nation to which Byron had sacrificed his life, France, Russia, and England, looked about for a young constitutional tyrant whom they might confer on their *protégée*.   Napoleon III. had at that epoch the casting vote in the council, and men were asking themselves anxiously whether he would put forward a candidate, and whether that candidate would be a Frenchman.   Briefly, the newspapers were full of stories about, and comments on this absorbing subject: the Greek question was the question of the hour.   The newsmongers could fearlessly give free rein to their imagination, for whilst the other nations seemed to have fixed their definite choice on

the son of the King of Denmark, the emperor
—so justly named "the taciturn prince" by the
friend of his dark days, Charles Dickens—
the emperor, I say, held his peace, and let
his decision be waited for.

Thus matters stood, when one morning
early in March the tall marquis burst like a
whirlwind into the dreary drawing-room in the
Rue St. Honoré brandishing a newspaper, and
in an indescribable state of excitement, soon
to be shared by all his family.   This was the
strange news registered that day in the
columns of several Parisian newspapers :
"We learn on good authority that a new
candidature has just been announced for the
throne of Greece.   The candidate this time
is a French grand seigneur well known all
over Paris—the Comte Philippe Auguste
de Villiers de l'Isle Adam, last descendant of
the august line which has produced the heroic
defender of Rhodes and the first Grand Master
of the Knights of Malta.   At the emperor's
last private reception, one of his intimates
having inquired concerning the probability of
this candidate's success, his majesty smiled

enigmatically. The new aspirant to kingly honours has our best wishes."

Those who have followed me so far will easily imagine the effect produced on imaginations like those of the Villiers family by such a perusal. Already they beheld their Matthias entering Athens, dressed in black velvet, proudly seated on a white charger, surrounded by his splendid *Palikares!*

As for Matthias himself, he took it all very seriously, though he doubted of ultimate success.

"Sire!" said the old marquis gravely, as he majestically buttoned his coat, worn white with wear, "money is the one thing you want! Your majesty's father will see you get it! Farewell! I am going to see Rothschild!"

He went, and was seen no more for a week.

But let me quickly explain the origin of this extraordinary adventure. It might truly be called the hoaxer hoaxed, with the qualification, however, that the hoaxee would never believe in a hoax at all.

In the days when Villiers was the chief figure of the little circle at the Rue de Douai and of some literary *caboulets* (as were then called certain cafés where writers congregated), he had a rival, a splendid fellow with pale skin, eagle eyes, and a thick black head of hair, whom the Parnassians nicknamed " Le Lion de Numidie," although he only hailed from Montpellier. I will call him by no other name, for since those days the lion has clipped his mane, cut his claws, and done public penance to society! Gifted with a wonderful constitution, with delightful spirits and good temper, with a much-dreaded shrewdness and surprising powers of observation, this jolly Colossus would have been invulnerable, had he not been afflicted with a vanity as strange as it was unwarrantable.

The Numidian lion had pretensions to being an admirable actor, and never lost an opportunity of showing off his talent for mimicry and his powers of declamation. Villiers, who had already practised that terrible, cold, and serious irony, which makes all the weaknesses of human nature its target, soon perceived the weak place in his jolly boon companion's armour. He longed for a

joke, insinuated himself into the lion's good
graces, and by degrees succeeded in putting
him off his guard.   He then explained to him
that some friends of his were desirous of
playing the " Moor of Venice " on a stage hired
for that purpose, but that they could find no
one capable of undertaking the part of Othello,
and the more so as it was absolutely necessary, to keep the local colour, that the actor
should stain his face and arms black.   " Don't
let that hinder you," cried his friend boldly ;
" I am your man ; here is my hand on it !"
With astonishing patience and gravity, Villiers
helped his friend to rehearse, and told him
where to get " made up."   Then a dress
rehearsal was called, to take place at the
usual trysting-place of the band of poets.   I
need not say there never had been a question
of playing Shakespeare's masterpiece, but,
all the same, Villiers had summoned all the
poets, " horse, foot, and dragoon."   When
Othello, in his splendid dress, his hands and
face as black as those of the King of Dahomey,
made his entrance, a general shout went up at
the sight of the Numidian lion, who richly

justified his title.   The Provençal was too
sharp not to perceive at once that he had
been duped.   He took it well, and was the
first to laugh at his own strange get-up, but
anyone who intercepted the look with which
he favoured the descendant of the Grand
Master of the Order of Malta could have
foretold his speedy revenge.   He remained
Villiers' friend, and in his turn discovered
the defect in *his* coat of mail.   Then it was
that he laid a snare for his vanity, his patri-
cian pride, his foolish family pretensions,
which almost betokened genius.   The son of
the treasure-seeker was to be seduced by the
mirage of the throne and royal crown then
sparkling on the horizon !   The perpetrator of
the hoax had made his calculations admirably :
the candidature of Villiers de l'Isle Adam
could not seem anything abnormal to the
public.   The name was illustrious and high-
sounding ; it was not impossible, therefore,
that the sovereign, desirous of placing on the
Greek throne a monarch who owed everything to him, might choose amongst the
flower of the French nobility a person on

whom he designed to bestow a crown. The thing only became improbable, laughable, and grotesque, when one knew the two chief personages, the king, and the king's father.

Many people were taken in, and the expectant king soon received the usual avalanche of begging letters.

Our Matthias did not remain idle, nor dally with his golden dream. This throne which glistened with gems and precious stones through the blue smoke-clouds of his cigarette, tempted him much more than he acknowledged to himself. Instigated by his good friends, who were laughing at him in their sleeves, he drew up a request for an audience, and sent it to the Tuileries. Some days afterwards, a magnificent *estafette* drew up before the house in the Rue St. Honoré, and gave to the astonished *concierge* a letter sealed with the imperial arms, and addressed to the Comte Villiers de l'Isle Adam; the audience was granted, and fixed for an early date.

For the first and only time in his life, the poet found a tailor who gave him credit. He

ordered a sumptuous evening coat, with all its
appendages, and then he shut himself up in
his own room, to study before the glass his
entry, his gestures, and the speech which he
would address to the sovereign.

On his side, the terrible Southern, in whose
ear Nemesis ceaselessly whispered, did not
lose his time. Every day one or two newspapers contained some paragraph concerning
the "French candidate." It was announced
that the emperor was about to receive him:
it was related that his father, the marquis,
had had a long and cordial interview with
Baron Rothschild. But where the Numidian
lion really showed the wisdom of the serpent,
was in his manner of preparing his victim for
the impending audience. The writer, who was
then in the throes of his novel, "Isis," had
his imagination filled with those gloomy adventures which give such a romantic and
mysterious colour to the history of Italian
principalities in the sixteenth century. He
dreamt of nothing but palaces full of murderous
snares, whose walls opened, whose ceilings
descended, whose floors gaped, to stifle or en-

tomb the imprudent mortals who allowed themselves to be allured into the luxurious and fatal dwellings of tyrants and princes. The contriver of the trick took admirable advantage of the predisposition of his victim; he reminded him that the familiars of the Tuileries were not over-scrupulous; he told him a heap of tragic anecdotes relating to the morrow of the second of December, and having as their scene this palace, which, according to him, was as full of trap-doors as an operatic stage. Many people, he insinuated, who had entered that little door on the Place du Carrousel have never been seen to come out; so let Villiers beware, for if any favourite had an interest in his disappearance, a trap-door, a dungeon, might open suddenly under his feet. Above all, he must absolutely refuse to explain himself to any but the emperor himself!

At last the great day came, and poor Matthias, very pale and agitated in his brand-new clothes, got into a hired carriage, and drove away to the Tuileries; before starting, he made his will, and sent it to my father.

It is difficult to tell exactly what passed at the Tuileries : Villiers' version is so impressed with romance that it is not easy to disentangle the real from the imaginary. What seems certain is that the poet was received by the Duc de Bassano, who at that time fulfilled the functions of Grand Chamberlain of the Palace. Doubtless the old diplomatist tried to fathom Matthias's intentions by clever questioning, but he found himself confronted by a personage unlike any he had ever met in his long and adventurous career. As for the poet, his already heated imagination soon carried him into oblivion of his present whereabouts, to believe himself the hero of one of those dark and mysterious court intrigues, the dramatic histories of which he had lately been perusing. He refused to utter, would scarcely put his foot down without insulting precautions, responded coldly to the advances of his interlocutor, upon whom he cast glances and deeply significant smiles which were quite unintelligible to the chamberlain, and finally stated, courteously but firmly, that he was resolved to speak to nobody but the emperor himself.

"I must ask you, then, to take the trouble of coming another time, count," said the duke, rising; "his majesty is engaged, and commissioned me to receive you."

There is no doubt that the chamberlain took the man of genius for a lunatic, and, in spite of my admiration for the author of "L'Eve Future," I cannot wonder at it. Villiers used to relate that he was escorted through the apartments to the staircase by two muscular and threatening fellows dressed in black, and that he expected every moment to be cast into a dungeon. "For," he would add, "I saw, the instant I entered, that Bassano had been gained over to the son of the King of Denmark, and that his object in summoning me to the Tuileries was to get rid of an inconvenient and dangerous rival; but my coldness, my dignity, the good style and moderation of my words, doubtless impressed the Sbirri, and I was allowed to depart in peace."

The claimant went home with hanging head, in great terror of the secret police, fancying he was going to be arrested, thrown into prison, and perhaps put to death.

G

He barricaded himself into his room, and
never left it for a week.   At last the newspapers put an end to his anxieties and his
ambitious hopes, by announcing the final
nomination of his fortunate rival, the second
son of King Christian IX., who ascended
the throne of Greece under the title of
George I.

The last act of the comedy had been played
out, the curtain fell, but the principal actor
never would believe that it was all mere fancy.
He never doubted but that he had had the
most serious chance of success; and to the
last day of his life he would describe, in his
picturesque and glowing conversation, the
splendid things that he would have accomplished, if fortune had favoured him, and he
had become king.

Reader, you may laugh! but yet, would
much harm have been done? would the
Greeks have been less happy, if a gentle poet
had borne the sceptre of the country which
saw Aphrodite's immortal beauty rise from
the sparkling, foam-crested sea-waves—the
country of Homer, of Æschylus, of Anacreon,

of Aristophanes? Doubtless, the reign of Matthias would not have resembled that of our late highly-respectable Louis Philippe, but perhaps, fired by his genius, the Greece of Miltiades and Themistocles, of Marathon and Salamis, might have felt her ancient soul stir within her! The poet's kingdom is not alas! of this world, and his crown is a thorny one. And what, indeed, is a throne that it should be so eagerly desired? The hero of this adventure has told us in some very beautiful lines: let them form the conclusion of this veracious history.

> " Un trône pour celui qui rêve,
> Un trône est bien sombre aujourd'hui.
> Faîte des vanités humaines,
> A ses pieds saignent bien des haines,
> Souvent il voile bien des peines !
> La foule obscure reste au seuil :
> Sapin couvert d'hermines blanches.
> Il a sceptre et lauriers pour branches ;
> Il est formé de quatre planches
> Absolûment comme un cercueil ! " [1]

[1] "To him whose life is full of dreams
A throne is now a dreary seat.
Summit of earthly vanity,
By bloody hatreds girt about,

The old aunt, Mdlle. Kerinou, never rose from the great canopied bed in which I saw her at the end of that memorable year, for the first and only time in my life. Her pure and simple soul took wing to the gardens of Paradise, escorted by all her hopes and illusions. The departure of the good old lady was a terrible event for the Villiers de l'Isle family; up to now, thanks to her income, it had been possible to pursue the jog-trot journey of life without too many jolts, but her fortune, being for the most part in an annuity, necessarily died with her, and at her death these poor Bretons, exiled in cruel, terrible Paris, saw the ghost of penury rise up before them. The dwelling in the Rue St. Honoré was given up, and the furniture sold. The marquise went back to the country, in the hope of raising some funds; the marquis was *a quia*. He had (in connection with a wild society for

> It cloaks full oft the bitterest griefs,
> Unrecked of by the common herd.
> It's like some ermine-covered pine,
> Whose branches crown and sceptre make,
> And coffin-like, the thing is built,
> Hollow, and formed of planks of wood!"

working some problematic bitumen lakes) made acquaintance with the police court. I hasten to add that he left it with head erect and clean hands, but his pockets were utterly empty. Father and son separated, and Villiers went to live alone, to begin that sad pilgrimage through Parisian lodging-houses, which lasted all his life, and closed in the Rue Oudinot, under the roof of the Brotherhood of St. Jean de Dieu.

Soon after, I left Paris and the Collège Rollin, where I had completed my studies, to enter an English university. For me, too, the battle of life was beginning. Thenceforward I only heard of Villiers from time to time. I used to read his books, which he sent to my father, and often the newspapers reported his eccentricities and his deep sayings to me. On that interior stage which we all bear within us, and which men call memory, he appeared to me as a legendary personage, full of strange attraction, and I liked to make my father tell me every story he knew about our cousin Matthias.

. Certainly I little thought then, that these recollections and anecdotes would help me in my riper age to call up and bring to life the genial figure of the great Breton artist.

Neither did I suspect that, some years later, this great artist would become my own most revered teacher, my surest, most faithful, and most precious friend. But so it was to be. During three years, from 1877 to 1880, we lived side by side in an absolute and constant intellectual intimacy.   And if, even now, the love of the ideal and of the imperishably beautiful consoles me for much that is horrible, much that is wretched, much that is mediocre and unworthy, it is to Villiers de l'Isle Adam that I owe it; he it is, who, on those dark nights, when our feet trod the mud of Lutetia, eloquently pointed out to me the starry way.

In order then to conclude these notes, it remains for me to relate that part of the poet's life of which I was the almost daily witness.

CHAPTER VI.

My return to Paris—The Hôtel d'Orléans—My search
for Villiers — Our reunion — The earlier stages
of his lawsuit—The historical drama of "Perrinet
Leclerc" — Paul Clèves, director of the Porte
St. Martin Theatre—The Maréchal Jean de l'Isle
Adam, according to Messrs. Lockroy and Anicet
Bourgeois—Villiers' fury—Letters to the press—A
summons—A memorandum—Intervention of M. de
Villiers—Provocation—A duel arranged—Settlement
on the ground—Result of the action—Biographer's
reservations—Documentary evidence.

OWARDS the autumn of 1876, at
the close of a long journey in
Switzerland, I returned to Paris,
my eyes still dazzled by the
glamour of virgin snows, inaccessible peaks,
glistening glaciers, and the great blue lake
wherein melancholy Chillon reflects its gloomy
keep. Through that land of mountain, fir-

wood, and torrent, the spirit of my father, whose death I yet mourned, had been with me everywhere, teaching me the better to appreciate and admire the sublimity of those landscapes for which he had always had a sort of passionate fondness. My entry into France was still haunted by the paternal presence, and I hurried to the old Hôtel d'Orléans, where we had spent so many years together, while I, alas! was too young and frivolous to profit by the counsels of that wise and generous mind. Whether it was by chance, or by a delicate attention on the part of the old host of the inn, I know not, but I was given my father's old room, and my first night was haunted by the shadows of the past. During those silent watches I lived through many an episode of my schoolboy days again, and many familiar faces passed before my eyes, some faintly looming in the shadow and as quickly disappearing, others clearly outlined and constantly recurring. Amongst these last, the big fair head of Villiers de l'Isle Adam constantly reappeared, his eyes seeming to gaze on me intently, and to reproach me with my

long neglect.   Ah, no ! I had not, indeed,
forgotten him.   But the adventures and wor-
ries of life had up to this prevented me from
seeking him out, and, since the childish days
already referred to, I had never beheld him.
But I resolved not to leave Paris this time
without finding him, and binding our two
selves together with bonds as strong and as
affectionate as those which had once united
him and my father.

The next evening, before the dinner hour,
I sought him along the boulevard.   Every
habitué, every lounger, from the Café de la
Paix to the Café de Madrid, knew Villiers de
l'Isle Adam, but nobody knew where he lived,
nor could tell where he might be found.   He
was, so they said, peculiarly a night-bird, and
almost all those who mentioned him to me had
made his acquaintance at unearthly hours,
in out-of-the-way *brasseries*.   None of this
information was of much service to me, and I
was beginning rather to despair, when a sudden downpour of rain drove me to take refuge
in the entry of the Passage Gouffroy.   I was
mechanically watching the play of light and

shade caused by the shower, when suddenly, and without an instant's hesitation, in spite of the lapse of years, in spite of the change which the fight for existence had wrought in his appearance, I recognized him! There are some strong individualities which age, care, even sickness, cannot alter. They are un-changeable. And Villiers was one of these.

He was coming into the passage from the rear, a big bundle of manuscript under his arm, with that elastic yet hesitating tread I so well remembered, taking quick, short steps, looking preoccupied and flurried at once, as he passed through the throng.

Poor great poet! judging by his hat, which was worn red with age, the thin threadbare frock-coat which concealed his shirt, the trousers with their frayed hem, Fortune, that jade, had treated him with condign scorn. What matter! As he came towards me, I read neither discouragement nor despair upon his ageing features. There was the same pale uncertain blue eye, lost in its dream, and beneath the fair moustache, already turning grey, the full mouth smiled as at some secret vision. He was, in good sooth, far from earth at that moment, and there seemed to me something proud and noble, amidst that jostling, pushing crowd of wet, muddy, common-looking passers-by, in the scornful indifference of the great thinker to the human rabble through which he passed, all unseeing, like the sleepwalker of some oriental tale.

As he drew near to me, the memory of our first meeting in the dining-room of the old house at Fougères came back to me, and touching his shoulder gently, I addressed him with a slight variation of the words he used when he found me, a child in disgrace, eating my solitary breakfast at the deserted family board: "Good morning, cousin! you don't know me. I am your cousin Robert!"

He started like a man suddenly roused from sleep, and raised his eyes to mine. His usually lustreless glance brightened ; we fell into each other's arms, and embraced shamelessly *coram populo*. Doubtless Heaven smiled on our reunion, for the setting sun was making the wet pavements and roofs shine again, as arm in arm we went out upon the boulevards.

It was during that first evening's converse, which cemented the friendship of our manhood's years, that Villiers de l'Isle Adam recounted to me the earlier stages of the strange action which he was about to bring against the Lockroy family and the heirs of the melodramatic playwright, Anicet Bourgeois — a most fantastic lawsuit, which amused and interested all Paris for several months, and of which I desire now to relate the apparently improbable incidents.

It happened, then, one winter evening in 1876, that my cousin Matthias was dreaming along the Boulevard du Crime, when, as he passed before the Porte St. Martin Theatre, its façade, lighted up as it usually was on important occasions, attracted his attention. He drew near to the advertisement boards, and started on seeing, below the title of the play of which a reproduction was to be given that night, "Perrinet Leclerc," an historical drama in five acts, by Messrs. Lockroy and Anicet Bourgeois, the name of his own illustrious ancestor, the Marshal Jean de Villiers de l'Isle Adam, occupying a line by itself.

"What!" roared the poet, "they have put the glorious marshal on the stage unknown to me? Ha! ha! We'll have some fun!" and he hastened to the box office.

The Porte St. Martin Theatre was at that time under the management of a very worthy fellow of the name of Paul Clèves, who had been in his time a good actor, and who, though not literary himself, was full of respectful admiration for the literary merits of others. He had a reverence not unmixed with awe for the eccentric genius of Villiers, and the moment he saw him he hurried with outstretched hands to meet him and place him in the managerial box, so that he might not lose a word nor a gesture of the actor personifying that famous warrior whose descendant the poet was. But, after the second act, Villiers reappeared in the unfortunate Clèves' private room, pale, trembling, and bristling with fury. "Sir!" he cried, with a tragic gesture, "two ignorant and conceited clowns, Lockroy and Bourgeois, have endeavoured to degrade one of the most illustrious warriors of the fourteenth century, whose name it is my glory to bear, and whose reputation it is my duty to defend! *You* have allowed this infamy to be committed, and I call upon *you*, sir, to withdraw the play to-morrow."

"But, my dear Villiers, it is impossible!" cried Clèves, when he had recovered from his profound astonishment, "consider! it would be my ruin. It would be certain bankruptcy! my engagements——"

"Ruin, bankruptcy, engagements! These are nothing to me. You should have warned me before you accepted this nonsensical stuff."

"I never accepted it. It has been in the repertory since 1834!"

"Enough, sir. I understand you to refuse? Very good, I shall apply to the authors—the authors, I say. Where are the authors?"

"They are dead!"

"Well for them! But they must have left children, heirs, representatives. That cur, that Simon, whose name is not even Lockroy, has a descendant who has made stir enough in this third Republic of yours! Well, we shall see! For the last time, Clèves, do you refuse to withdraw the play?"

The unlucky manager had become speechless, but he made a sign with his head which seemed to signify that it was impossible to grant such a request.

"Very well, then," said the poet, "you and your accomplices shall hear from me!" And he went out in a fury.

Those who can recollect Villiers de l'Isle Adam's idolatrous worship for the memory of his ancestors will understand this outbreak of rage when I state that this unlucky so-called historical drama by Messrs. Lockroy and Bourgeois represented the Maréchal de l'Isle Adam as a disloyal nobleman and an abominable traitor—traitor, not in favour of the Duke of Burgundy, nor of the Duke of Orleans, but traitor to his own country, to his poor mad king, delivering both over to the English power, and aiding Henry V. to place upon his own head the crown torn from that of the rightful sovereign. All this was absolutely contrary to the truth. Jean de l'Isle Adam, the friend and right-hand man of the Duke

of Burgundy, was, it is true, the most ardent
partisan of John the Bold, and took possession
of Paris in his name. As to the English,
Jean refused the splendid offers of Henry V.,
who cast him into the Bastille, whence he
only emerged after that prince's death.
Thenceforward he warred ceaselessly against
the British, from whom he recaptured Pon-
toise in 1435. Such are the historical facts
of the case. But the authors of " Perrinet
Leclerc" cared little for that. To those
makers of melodramas, history was but a
mine to supply their own lack of imagination, and its personages merely obliging
dummies, to be dressed up in glory or
infamy, according to the needs of their case.
They wanted a traitor, and they simply took
Villiers de l'Isle Adam, in all good faith,
never dreaming that there would appear, five
hundred years after the fulfilment of the
events they were putting on the stage, in this
fin-de-siècle and gaping Paris of ours, a poet
who was ready to make himself the champion
and the vigorous defender of his outraged
ancestor !

Never did Villiers show such activity, such physical and moral energy, as in the course of this business. For my own part, my knowledge of him leads me to the opinion that, in spite of all his indignation, he rather enjoyed the adventure. The excitement of the judicial struggle, the newspaper polemics, the ransacking of libraries both far and near, put a new interest into his life, and freed his mind for a while from the dreams which so incessantly haunted it. And that arch-scoffer must have felt a curious secret amusement in obliging all that army of solicitors, barristers, judges, and their deputies, to occupy themselves with the affairs of an illustrious old gentleman who had been dead for four hundred and fifty years, to decipher the quaint and incomprehensible manuscripts of the thirteenth century, and to busy themselves, under the reign of Grévy, Wilson, and Co., with the concerns of Charles VI. the Bienaimé, of John the Bold, and of the fatally fascinating Isabeau of Bavaria.

But to begin at the beginning. The very morning after that memorable performance,

H

there appeared in several daily papers a haughty and indignant letter from the last of the De l'Isle Adams, in which he brilliantly vindicated his right to defend his illustrious relative from opprobrium. He blasted in a few scorching phrases, conceived in ineffable scorn for all dealers in such second-hand literary wares, the work of the two unlucky collaborators; and he finally declared that he was about to appeal to the laws of the country to obtain for them the chastisement of their crime of treason against the national glory. There was much giggling along the boulevards at the poet's new freak. The collateral heirs of the acting rights of the play turned a deaf ear to his threat, and "Perrinet Leclerc" still held the bills, its success much increased by this fresh puff. Forward, then, the officers, the formalities, the dusty papers, all the creaking machinery of the law! A clever and intelligent young barrister, an acquaintance of Villiers, eagerly seized on this opportunity of distinguishing himself; for this action was to stir both the law courts and the boulevards, and those who had to do with it soon became famous.

The representatives of Lockroy and of Anicet Bourgeois had to file their answer to the summons duly served upon them—a summons praying that they might be forbidden to continue the performances of a play wherein they libelled and calumniated the direct ancestor of the plaintiff, "the said Philippe Auguste Matthias de Villiers de l'Isle Adam, man of letters, which summons has been personally delivered at the defendants' house. Herewith a copy, whereof the price," etc., etc., etc.

The defendants' answer was rather clever. They asked the tribunal to rule that the plaintiff's plea was inadmissible : firstly, because he offered no proof of his boasted direct descent from the illustrious house of Villiers de l'Isle Adam ; secondly, because the chronicles of the time, and notably that of the Monk of St. Denis, authorized the writers of " Perrinet Leclerc " in presenting the conduct of the Marshal de l'Isle Adam during the civil wars of the reign of Charles VI. in an unfavourable light ; thirdly, because the said Marshal de l'Isle Adam being an historical personage, any writer might criticise or praise him, according to conscience or personal opinion, without being liable to any action on that score.   Thus the fight began.

And now, for some weeks, Matthias was undiscoverable.   He buried himself in the libraries and the archives, amongst which his clear mind called up all that gloomy and romantic period which began at the infancy of Charles VI. and ended on the day when Jeanne d'Arc led the weak-kneed Charles VII. to Rheims, to be anointed king.   When the lawsuit began, nothing remained to Villiers of the family inheritance.   Pressed by poverty, father and son had parted with everything; but they still preserved the precious family archives, and the poet possessed irrefragable proof of his descent.

When, therefore, he had sufficiently studied the formidable heap of documents bearing on the ten years of civil war which stained the close of the reign of Charles VI., he prayed leave to support his request against the authors of " Perrinet Leclerc " : firstly, by the proof, resting on authentic records, of his descent from that Marshal de l'Isle Adam whose

honour he claimed to defend ; secondly, by
proving that no contemporary chronicler gave
to his ancestor that odious character which
Messrs. Lockroy and Bourgeois had dared to
make him play in the history of his time.
And, he added, if it was true that the so-called
Chronicle of the Monk of St. Denis did contain a sentence which permitted any doubt on
that score, it was established, on the other
hand, that these memoirs had no character
for authenticity, that they were held in suspicion by all competent historians, and that,
in any case, it was sufficient to read the manuscript to be convinced that it was a partial
work, and that its author belonged to that
faction which was hostile to the Duke of
Burgundy, the friend of De l'Isle Adam.

To this second appeal Villiers added a long
memorandum, addressed to the judges.   I do
not know what has become of this manuscript.
I hope that those persons who have undertaken, with so much zeal and devotion, the
posthumous publication of the works of the
author of " Axël," may have it in their possession.   In it the great writer appears in a

new light. This sketch of the life of the Marshal de l'Isle Adam is a masterpiece of clearness and style, a gifted and magnificent word-picture of the end of the thirteenth century, a strong and closely-reasoned piece of work, in which the fervent eloquence of his pleading for the thesis he defends never fetters the critical and investigating faculty of its author.

Thus matters stood when I joined Villiers in Paris. The adversaries were armed at all points, and only waited the close of the vacation to go before the courts.

All at once, an unexpected event, a tragi-comic incident, gave a fresh interest to the affair.

I have related, in the early pages of these recollections, how a family bearing the name of Villiers, but which had shown no proof of direct descent from the Grand Master of the Knights of Malta, had been authorized, at the time of the return of the Bourbons, to add the name of L'Isle Adam to its own patronymic. Just as our Villiers was emerging from his tent, armed *cap à pié*, and lance in rest, to defend his ancestral glory and good fame against the calumnies of two playwrights, the representative of this other family, a young officer, very proud of the great name he bore, and exceedingly ignorant, as it seems, of his real origin, returned from Africa. Honestly believing himself the scion of those heroes who had shed glory on the name of De l'Isle Adam, his rage and stupefaction may be imagined when, hardly had he arrived home, ere his friends and relations placed before him various newspapers, which reported with much comment, and wit seasoned with Attic salt, the particulars of the action brought by the high-born poet against the guilty authors of " Perrinet Leclerc." Incredible as it seems in these days, when the press penetrates everywhere, the young warrior appears to have ignored till then the existence of one of the best-known literary men in Paris. He fancied the author of " Isis " to be some scribbling adventurer who had picked up for himself, out of history, a name which he believed to be extinct. In the heat of his indignation, he wrote a letter to a great daily paper, and as the

officer knew more about the cavalry sword-
exercise than about the amenities of our
beautiful French language, his communication
was at once plain-spoken, rude, and aggres-
sive, claiming his right to bear the name of
Villiers de l'Isle Adam, and avowing that
any other person calling himself by that
name usurped it.   This warlike missive soon
appeared, and forthwith all the venomous
small fry of the press, all the envious scrib-
blers, all the failures whom Villiers' talent
had overshadowed, and whom his bitter jests
had wounded, pounced upon this lucky wind-
fall.   Along the boulevards, from the Made-
leine to the Gymnase, at the hour of the
absinthe queen, their little poisonous speeches
were to be heard on every side : " That poor
Villiers ! Don't you know ?—Not De l'Isle
Adam at all !—It was a name he took !—*I*
always thought so !—It seems he is really the
son of a small grocer at Guingamp."

Ah ! why cannot we sear the lips of slan-
derers with a red-hot iron ? Shame on those
dastards ! for this time at least they managed
to pierce my friend to the heart. All those

who knew him well, knew that beneath his
strange exterior and his cold mask of scorn
Villiers had a noble ardent soul, which must
have suffered cruelly under the thousand
anonymous stings which were inflicted on his
pride.   But the blood of the marshal and the
grand master boiled in his veins, and on the
very day of the insult the officer was waited
upon by two poet-friends of the writer, who
came from the Comte Philippe Auguste de
Villiers de l'Isle Adam to demand reparation
for the outrage offered to their principal.
The adversary was brave, and accepted
without flinching the meeting which was
proposed to him ; and the seconds having
conferred, it was arranged that all should go,
armed with swords, the day after the next
following, on a little expedition to the neigh-
bourhood of Vésinet.   Meanwhile, one of the
seconds of Matthias, a sensible man, though
a violent Parnassian, struck by the exceedingly correct demeanour of the other party,
thought it might not be altogether useless to
submit to him certain genealogical proofs
which would demonstrate to him that right

was not altogether on his side, as he fancied. After a severe struggle he induced Villiers to lend him those famous and precious family documents for the space of twenty-four hours, and sent them to the cavalry lieutenant with an urgent request that he would read them before the hour fixed for the meeting. The result was amazing. M. de Villiers was a loyal, good-hearted, and very chivalrous man. He appeared on the ground at the appointed hour, advanced towards the real Villiers de l'Isle Adam, made him a bow, and offered him the most courteous apology, adding that it was only on the preceding evening that he had learnt the truth. It was worth hearing Villiers, with his tragic gestures, and the perpetual wagging of his front fair lock, retail the incidents of this *coup de théâtre*. "Sir!" he would cry, "my sword dropped from my hand, when I heard this pale young man, with his brave and resigned face, tell me, with an evident effort, that, French officer as he was, he would rather pass for a coward than fight in support of a lie. I opened my arms. I folded him to my heart. I told him he was worthy to be allied with the illustrious dead whose representative I was; and in my father's name and my own, I authorized, nay, I besought him to continue to bear the name of Villiers de l'Isle Adam!"

But everything, even lawsuits, must come to an end; and one fine morning the judges gave their decision in the extraordinary case of "L'Isle Adam *versus* Simon, *alias* Lockroy, and Anicet Bourgeois." As my reader will be prepared to learn, the tribunal refused the poor poet's appeal, deeming it inadmissible because, as the marshal was historical property, every author had a right to show him in whatever light suited him best; especially when he based his judgment, as in the case of the writers of "Perrinet Leclerc," on the evidence of contemporary documents and memoirs, such as the Chronicle of the Monk of St. Denis. But one consolation Villiers had. The preamble of the judgment established those direct ties of descent which made him the last representative of that famous and heroic warrior who was the friend of the great Duke of Burgundy.

When I learnt these events from the poet's lips, they were already in the limbo of the past.

Were I not possessed with an instinctive and not altogether unreasonable horror of foot-notes, I would inflict one on my readers, *à propos* to this trial, to state that I have related the whole of it from recollection—a recollection graven upon my memory by the picturesque recitals of my gifted and much regretted cousin. In thus summing up, without actually vouching for the facts of the story, I trust I have not trangressed in any particular against the truth. But in any case I shall be very glad to accept any verification which may be kindly submitted to me.

I think further, that I shall do no prejudice to the memory of Villiers, if I frankly confess that I entertain some serious doubt concerning the alleged handsome retraction made by his opponent on the scene of the intended duel. The poet was in the habit of dramatizing all the incidents of his daily life into enchanting stories. Their groundwork was generally true, but he would arrange the scene, invent incidents, and create personages, in obedience apparently to his æsthetic instinct, or perhaps rather to his wild innate longing to mystify his audience.   In this particular case my suspicion is supported by the following succinct and nobly-expressed letter, addressed to him by his adversary, and which, necessarily, put an end to their difference.   At all events this document proves that our author was in the right.

                "Paris,
                  "*February* 16*th*, 1877.

"SIR,

    " I can only bow before the incontestably authentic title-deeds which you have been so good as to communicate to me, and which indeed establish unanswerably your descent from that family of Villiers de l'Isle Adam whose name is written in such glorious characters upon the pages of our history, and in whose ranks figures the Marshal Jean, whose memory, in spite of what anyone may say, remains above all suspicion.

    " This does not, however, alter the fact that

a royal ordinance, dated September 7, 1815, and inserted in the ' Bulletin des Lois,' authorizes my grandfather, Vicomte Joseph-Gabriel, son of François-Ignace de Villiers des Champs, and of Dame Désheré le Borgue de Villement, his wife, to add to his name of Villiers that of De l'Isle Adam.

" There appears to me to be no object to be gained by going into the genealogy of my family, which has given knights and commanders to the Order of St. Louis and marshals to France,—which is allied to the Rohans, etc., etc.

" And, in conclusion, if, contrary to my expectations, the explanations contained in this letter do not appear to you to suffice, pray be assured that I hold myself entirely at your disposal.

(*Signed*) " G. VILLIERS DE L'ISLE ADAM."

While I am about quoting the documents bearing on this curious business, the reader may be glad that I should conclude by giving the principal passages of the fine letter written by Villiers to the newspapers of the day, in

answer to the mean and spiteful attacks of
which he was then the object.

.

     "Paris (undated, probably *January*, 1877).

   "To the Editor of . . . .

"SIR,

     "This is my answer to the article you
have published concerning me. I desire that
it may suffice for all those of your colleagues
of the press, who have been good enough to
devote their precious time to me, and busy
themselves with my name, during the past
week.

     "It has been claimed that my sole object
in bringing an action against the proprietors
of the play 'Perrinet Leclerc,' was to establish
the genealogical succession of my own family.
Now I may remark that for eight-and-thirty
years I committed the grave indiscretion of
never giving that question a thought, believing it (with others whose duty calls them to
consider it) so clearly established that I could
afford to smile at any discussion of the subject. I may further remark that it was only

the request of counsel on the other side which obliged me to produce any such proofs at all. It seems strange, then, that this reproach should be made to me by the very adversaries who attacked me on this point at the moment when I myself was about to desist from the struggle.

"It has been asserted that there is a gap in the sequence of my family genealogy. Now genealogy is an exact science, which no more admits of a mistake than does algebra. In it 'five centuries' mean nothing. They should have been described as 'twelve generations.'

"The records of the Order of Malta, in which the whole nobility of France and of Europe are concerned, are indisputable evidence all over the world, and that Order would not give a careless decision concerning the descendants of a Grand Master such as the one whose name I bear.

"That a clerk should write a 3 instead of a 9 on the hasty copy of a title of the order, and that (in spite of the opportunities given by me during two years for free and open investigation) such an error should be quoted against the absolute authoritativeness of my title-deeds, is, I repeat, merely a matter calculated to raise a smile. In any case, I shall bring the facts before the French Record Office.

"I descend from Jean de l'Isle Adam as directly as any of you gentlemen descends from his own father; and, in spite of the 'Chronique de St. Denis,' I have some reason to be proud of the fact.

"I am asked what interest I had in vexing my soul concerning a play which outrages his pure and sacred memory; and it is affirmed that I simply desired to puff myself by doing so. A man is but that which his own thoughts make him. And for my only answer, I would beg those who have had this thought concerning me, to guard it preciously. They are quite worthy of it, and I shall never care to claim either their sympathy or esteem. . . .

"There is as much truth in this assertion as in that which claims to have discovered a gap in the direct succession of my family about the year 1535. It is a wonderful thing to note how lightheartedly a lawyer will cast

I

doubt on the records of the Order of Malta, which are an article of faith to the nobility of the whole world; on the signed attestations whereby provincial bishops have recognized three centuries of publicly-admitted family rights; on the signatures of ambassadors and consuls, both French and English; and on that of the Minister of Justice himself!

"I have no right to submit myself to any legal investigation on this head. An investigation of what? Of my claims to be of noble descent? But the only course left to the law courts themselves must be to bow to those claims, which are established by the only tribunal to which I can in honour appeal. One alone, among the signatures with which these parchments swarm, suffices to prove my contention. The text of the 'Declaration of the Order of Malta' runs as follows: 'Notum facimus et in verbo veritatis attestamur ut in judicio pleno ac indubia fides adhibeatur. . . .

"'We declare under our seal and that of the Papal Bull published this day, that Armand de l'Isle Adam, admitted a knight of this

Order, has proved his quarterings in the most indisputable manner.

"'We, Caumartin, Intendant de Champagne, bear witness to the correctness of the genealogy of, etc., etc., etc.

"'We, Bishop of St. Brieuc, ourselves connected through the family of De Verdalle with the Knights of Malta, bear witness that for the last three hundred years it has been matter of public notoriety that, etc., etc., etc.'

"How can you expect any law court to pronounce for or against, in such a matter? How can any newspaper chatter affect it? Centuries have rolled by. You come in too late. These are accomplished facts!"

CHAPTER VII.

Le Pin Galant, near Bordeaux—Arrival of Villiers
with his play—"The New World"—The American
centenary competition—The character of Mistress
Andrews—The legend of Ralph Evandale.

HILE Villiers was thus struggling
with the gentlemen of the wig and
gown in the Paris law courts, I
followed his movements from afar
with considerable anxiety. In my retirement
in one of those pretty one-storied houses
near Bordeaux which the people in the south
poetically term a "Chartreuse," I trembled as
I tore asunder the wrapper of my Paris paper
every morning, lest I should learn that Villiers, whose fearfully over-excited condition
was well known to me, had given way to
some eccentricity or some dangerous act of
violence. I kept on writing to beseech him

to leave Paris, and to come and share my solitude, redolent of the healthy odour of the pine forests, enlivened by the impetuous rush of the great river dotted with white and fluttering sails, and ideal with its spreading horizons bathed in the purple and gold of the exquisite southern sunsets.

But, alas! he wrapped himself in disheartening silence, and his shadow fell not on the snow-white steps which led to the Pin Galant, as my temporary dwelling was called.

One day, however, the " Figaro " brought me news of his speedy arrival, in the form of a letter published on its first page, and bearing his signature. I have not this document before me, but I know that in it he refuted, in his usual sarcastic style, some fresh perfidious insinuation concerning the imperfect authenticity of the name he bore. The last sentence of the letter, however, which gave me a lively thrill of joy, is for ever graven on my memory. I quote it, as being exceedingly characteristic. " I am on the point of starting for Pin Galant, not far from the Spanish frontier. Lovers of another style of conversation, more silent than that of human tongues, are requested to note this fact."

He duly appeared a few days later, without having otherwise announced himself.

It was on one of those torrid afternoons known only to the inhabitants of the south, that Villiers arrived on foot from the neighbouring village, whither the omnibus from Bordeaux had brought him. He was simply dressed, in black kerseymere trousers, a loose grey overcoat trimmed with fur (!), and a well-worn but shiny chimneypot hat. In his hand he victoriously flourished a huge walking-stick. The big pockets of his unseasonably thick overcoat bulged in a manner which alarmed me for their solidity. At first I thought he was using them as a carpet-bag, for he brought no sign of any other luggage with him. But my mistake only lasted a few minutes. Hardly had he entered, when, after the first cordial greetings, he pulled out of his vast pockets five thick manuscript pamphlets, piling them one upon the other,

and his white, prelatical hand waving with
the air of a bishop a sort of benedictory
gesture, he exclaimed, "Like Columbus at
the feet of his Spanish sovereign, even so lay
I the 'New World' at the feet of your
majesty and my good cousin!" The books
contained, in good truth, the manuscript of
his magnificent drama in five acts, entitled
"Le Nouveau Monde," which had gained
the first place, the year before, in the competition instituted in honour of the United
States, but which had not yet found an
opening on the Parisian stage.

Before relating the adventures of Villiers
and his manuscript at Bordeaux, I think it
will be of interest to scholars if I give some
explanation of the origin of this dramatic
work, which, in spite of its admirable qualities,
is almost unknown at this present time. In
1880 Villiers de l'Isle Adam found a publisher bold enough to issue it at his own risk,
and his name deserves to be recorded. It
was M. Richard, printer and publisher, of
the Passage de l'Opéra. The pamphlet is
now almost out of print. Villiers had pre-

ceded his play by an "Address to the Reader," to which I shall return later, in its proper time and place, and by a very short preface, which I quote in its entirety, because it explains far better than I could the peculiar circumstances which gave birth to the work.

"In 1875 a dramatic competition was announced by the theatrical press of Paris. A medal of honour, even a sum of 10,000 francs, and other temptations, were offered to the French dramatic author who should most powerfully recall, in a work of four or five acts, the episode of the proclamation of the independence of the United States, the hundredth anniversary of which fell on July 4th, 1876.

"The two examining juries were thus composed. The first, of the principal critics of the French theatrical press. The second, of M. Victor Hugo, honorary president, Messrs. Emile Augier, Octave Feuillet, and Ernest Legouvé, members of the French Academy, Mr. Grenville Murray, representing the "New York Herald," and M. Perrin, administrator-general of the Théâtre Français.

" The preliminary jury were to select five manuscripts; the final jury, to class these manuscripts in what may be called their intellectual order.

" Six months were allowed for writing the works, and about a hundred plays, signed with mottoes only, were forwarded to the international agency of M. Théodore Michaëlis, the inaugurator of the competition.

" More than a year elapsed while the gentlemen of the theatrical press were examining the dramas.

" The titles of the selected works were published, and among them appeared that of the 'Nouveau Monde.'

" Two more months passed by. At last, on the 22nd of January, 1876, an official notice signed by the superior jury informed me that the 'Nouveau Monde,' had of all the competing works, passed with most honour through the double ordeal."

The attractions of the programme had been well arranged to tempt any dramatic author. Yet it was not the medal of honour, nor even the dream of the ten thousand

francs, which induced the creator of Bonhomet
to compete. It was the proposed subject;
above all, the conditions imposed for its treat-
ment. From the theatrical point of view,
Villiers had always dreamt of being an inno-
vator in historical drama. His idea was that
the characteristics of the nation, or the event
which was to be portrayed, should be imported into the framework of some personal
intrigue, in which each individual of the
dramatis personæ should personify in his language, attitude, or actions, some one of the
numerous elements produced by the friction
of the incidents of the story. And in the
very terms of the programme by which the
competitors were bound, he found the opportunity for realizing this conception. For the
rules of the competition dictated, amongst
other obligations, that the work must be
written with special reference to July 4th,
1776; at the same time requiring a *drame
intime*, in which the event of the 4th July
was only to be superadded to the story.

In the author's mind, then, " Le Nouveau
Monde" is, before all else, a symbolic drama,

and each of its personages admirably represents the idea, the principle, the nation, of
which he or she is the mouthpiece. Thus, in
Lord Raleigh Cecil the author has incarnated
the principle of royalism, as in Stephen
Ashwell he has typified the principle of
liberty. " In my play," writes Villiers in his
preface, " Lord Cecil, under a veil of almost
totally imaginary circumstances, replaces and
sums up Lord Percy, General Howe, and
many others. He is, as it were, the golden
sovereign, stamped with the effigy of the
King of England."

It is hardly my place, in these personal
recollections, to endeavour to heighten the
merits of this work of Villiers. But I may
be permitted to lay stress on some details of
an original production, so little known to the
literary public, and yet so worthy of its attention. To those of us who are not yet emas-
culated by the terrible invasion of commonplace ideas, " Le Nouveau Monde" remains
one of the best constructed, deepest, and most
passionate dramas of the present day. It
has had the great honour of being sneered at

by M. Francisque Sarcey, who has besprinkled
the character of Mistress Andrews with the
salt of his Attic wit.   To some superficial
minds this character may seem impressed
with romantic exaggeration.   Yet it has been
learnedly imagined and laboriously premedi-
tated by a writer who was neither a novice
nor a simpleton in literature.   Villiers fore-
saw that it would be exposed to the cheap
jests of those self-important gentry, the
critics of the weekly papers.   In his "Address
to the Reader" he has taken pains to explain
his conception, and this page of his, full of
an intense personality, so wonderfully and
rhythmically written, cannot fail to charm
my readers.   It seems to me it must
make every true artist desire to read that
"Nouveau Monde" so lately cut up by the
feuilletonists.   Here it is:

"Mistress Andrews is the sombre reflection
of that feudalism of which Lord Cecil represents the brighter side, and I find myself
obliged to say a few words in explanation of
the almost fantastic character with which she
is endued.   This woman's personality is

formed by the cohesion of intellectual and
sensitive elements of far too high an order to
be strictly human.   Some peculiarities of the
character seem to be ultra-feminine. Therefore, in order to legitimatize them in her
case, I have had to surround her with a
legendary halo, to make her a sort of
American Melusina.   It has appeared to me
to be logically indispensable to the vitality,
even the possibility, of the character, to
endow her with a mysterious mark, actually
imprinted in her flesh, a gory impress which
shall appear only at the hour of death,—
a sign, in fact, the heritage of the curse of
centuries, with the extraordinary horror of
which popular tradition surrounds her name.
I have desired thus to create the type of a
strange, stormy, embittered soul—the daughter
of a race haunted by melancholy, by silence,
and by fate.   A thousand shattered splen-
dours appear athwart this gloomy character,
even as mirrors and goblets would shiver,
and daggers flash, against the arras of an
ancient palace wherein some ducal orgy had
been held. This having been said, some excla-

mations in the part, antiquated ones, perhaps, explain and make themselves acceptable, pronounced as they are by a being of so peculiar a nature."

But what was that "mysterious mark actually impressed upon this woman's flesh," this gory print which was only to appear at the death hour? What "the legendary halo" which surrounds the terrible Mistress Andrews? An old woman, Mistress Noella, describes it by the light of a camp-fire, in the midst of the virgin forest of the New World. The splendidly-related legend, which was almost entirely suppressed in the shapeless performance of this fine play at the Théâtre des Nations, must be inserted here, for several good reasons: first, for the sake of the curious, for it is as good as unpublished; further, it is an admirable prose-poem, whose place is marked in the anthologies of the future; and finally, it is a wonderful example of the peculiar genius of Villiers de l'Isle Adam.

The few friends who have heard him recite it, pale, trembling, and haggard, under the

light of the midnight lamp—terrifying, and
terrified himself by his own story—will recall
as they read these lines the tragic and
infectious dread which he threw into his
declamation.

"One evening the knight Ralph Evandale,
returning to his castle from the Wars of the
Roses, heard on the mountain the sound of
singing in his ancestral halls. In coat of
mail and with lowered vizor he climbed the
stone staircase, marvelling at the festive
sounds. A thousand lamps shone on the
guests. His father, Fungh Evandale, was
celebrating his second marriage, and the
neighbouring barons, sitting round him,
pledged each other in friendly healths. From
the threshold Ralph beheld the newly-wedded
wife, white as her coronet of pearls; and in
the bride he recognized the pale girl whom
he had long loved in his secret soul. A hell-
born feeling rose in his heart. Silently he
closed the door, and disappeared. Meanwhile the songs had ceased. Leaning thought-
fully on her elbow, on the nuptial couch, the
young *châtelaine* watched her lord. The noble

thane unbuckled his sword before the great
hanging mirror, when suddenly the tapestry
was pushed back by a gauntletted hand.   It
was Ralph this time, with vizor raised.
Fungh turned, and, recognizing him, joyfully
stretched out his arms.   But the cruel son,
impelled by some foul demon, started forward, fell traitorously on his father, and
plunged his dagger in his throat, up to the
cross-hilt.   Fungh, stricken to death, instinctively put his hand on the wound ; then,
with a maledictory gesture, he laid his gory
fingers on the face of the unnatural son who
gazed unmoved upon his agony.   Ralph drew
himself up, his heart sullied by his crime,
and *his face branded with his father's blood.*
Then, bruising in his mailed hands the two
wrists of the widowed bride, he dragged
her, half-naked, dishevelled, her knees shaking
with terror, into the adjacent oratory, and
would have constrained the chaplain of the
old manor to bless, in that very hour, their
sacrilegious union.   Terrified though he
was, the priest gathered courage before the
altar, and would only utter a well-deserved

anathema.   Thus was the guilty marriage solemnized.   And the shadow fell upon their race!   They gave life to a posterity of demons, an accursed line of wicked men, who have rendered themselves illustrious on the earth by their crimes and their gloomy amours.   Now the race is extinct.   One girl only survives, and she destroyed her property and burnt her dwelling before she fled her country.   Where is she?   Nobody can tell! Nevertheless, she will be recognized in her last hour, for, since the terrible night when their young ancestress beheld the bloody hand on the face of the parricide, that accusing hand-print, graven on the flesh of the Evandales, has perpetuated itself from generation to generation.   They are conceived with that impress!   It is the law of their birth!   And whenever death strikes one of them, the sinister hand appears upon the brow of the unhappy being,—a ghostly, shining hand, which the everlasting night alone can efface! Pray then for Edith Evandale, the last of her race, unknown, forgotten!"

This Edith Evandale, it will have been

K

understood, is she who now conceals herself under the name of Mistress Andrews. As the old woman concludes her story, and while all are still bending forward in silent and breathless attention, the unhappy woman herself appears standing among them, the moonlight falling on her alone. "Yes," she says in a low despairing voice, "pray!"

CHAPTER VIII.

Villiers' rage against the members of the jury—Dramatic
scene at the house of Victor Hugo—Villiers leaves
Paris—The Bordeaux theatres—Godefrin, director
of the Théâtre Français—An extraordinary reading
—Little Mdlle. Aimée—Madame Aimée Tessandier.

MY quotations have carried me away,
and we are far from Bordeaux!
To return. When Villiers arrived,
he was more furious than ever
with Paris and the Parisians in general, and
with literary committees and theatrical mana-
gers in particular. This time it was no
longer " Perrinet Leclerc," nor the loss of his
lawsuit, which excited his rage, but the succession of injustices of which the " Nouveau
Monde " and its author had been the victims.
He had, indeed, received the official notice,
signed by the superior jury, and announcing

that his drama had taken the highest and most honourable place in passing through the twofold ordeal. It had received the praises of Victor Hugo, of Emile Augier and Octave Feuillet, of Ernest Legouvé even! and that was all. No medal of honour, much less the ten thousand francs! He was, it is true, too well acquainted with the side-scenes of life at this end of the century to feel much surprised at seeing the gold turn into dead leaves, but he had hoped that those who had instituted the competition would, at all events, have made some effort to have the play of their choice performed on some great Parisian stage. Nothing of the kind. A flood of benignant commonplace was the only answer to his inquiries and his imperious demands, and the gifted author of the "Nouveau Monde" had to undergo the humiliation (surely, in another life, it shall be reckoned in his favour!) of seeing the second-rate play of one of his fellow-competitors, M. Armand d'Artois, performed on the Paris boards, while his own slumbered in the manuscript boxes of the manager of the Porte St. Martin Theatre.

It would have been too much even for a
being gifted with more patience than my poor
Villiers possessed.

As a first step the poet went and made a
scandal at the Olympian abode of Victor
Hugo, in the Avenue de Clichy.   In the
presence of the usual body-guard, Vacquerie,
Lockroy, Catulle Mendès, and my late venerable compatriot, L——, he dared to accuse
the honorary president of the superior jury of
having been the first to break all the promises
signed with his august name.   He mentioned
the demigod's age to him, and made some allu-
sion to literary integrity in general.   L——,
who usually sat silent in these gatherings,
never opening his mouth except to cry
"Sabaoth!" unable to contain his fury,
angrily advanced towards the intruder, and
indignantly shaking the beautiful white curls
which framed his pallid face, he shot at the
blasphemer this eloquent apostrophe, which
Homer or Henri Monnier might have been
glad to take a note of : " Integrity, sir, is not
a question of age !" Slowly, with his uncertain glance, Villiers scanned the worthy

elder from head to foot, then gently answered, " No, sir, nor folly either ! " Then, leaving the startled *coterie*, horrified at his unlimited audacity, he hurried to the Porte St. Martin, snatched his manuscript from the secretary's claws, and at dawn next day, laden with the five thick copybooks containing his five acts, and without vulgar care for such a trivial thing as luggage, he took the through train to Bordeaux.

" Then at once," he said, as he brought the story of the adventures of his play to a close, " I bethought me of you, of the provinces, of vengeance. I dreamt of murder, of decentralization ! Don't you see what a splendid chance there is here for the manager of some provincial theatre, to be first to accept and mount and play a piece by the Comte Villiers de l'Isle Adam, which has been crowned by the approbation of a committee counting among its members those idols of middle-class lovers of literature, Legouvé, Feuillet, Augier, and Hugo ? But, in the first place, *is* there a theatre in Bordeaux ? "

" There are three," I replied, " without count-

ing the strollers' booths." Bordeaux did, in
fact, possess in those days three important
theatres : the Grand Theatre, which was devoted to operatic performances, the Théâtre
Louit, which had no particular line, and the
Théâtre Français, which was entirely given
up to comedy and drama.   The then manager
of the latter was a Parisian artiste, a good
actor, and an excellent administrator, possessed of great boldness, much insight, and
most reliable good taste.   He has since made
himself a name at the Café de Suède, and in
the theatrical world, as a most successful
organizer of provincial and dramatic tours.
He was then, and presumably is still, called
Godefrin. We had had some casual relations
with each other, and as soon as Villiers im-
parted his new project to me, I bethought me
of the director of the Théâtre Français of Bordeaux.   I wrote to him, therefore, making
known our idea and asking for an early interview. We had not long to wait. The answer
came, overflowing with enthusiasm for Villiers
and full of gratitude to myself, and the very
next evening found us sitting in the managerial

apartment. Villiers had been to the barber;
his well-curled moustache had a conquering
air, and he marched victoriously through the
streets of Bordeaux with his manuscript under
his arm. But, as the sequel will show, this
pretence of assurance concealed a horrible
state of nervousness; he was, in reality, as
agitated as a *débutante* who hears the call-
boy's bell for the first time. And yet there
was nothing inaccessible in the demeanour of
the impresario! He was still young, free
from any professional swagger, and very
affable. He received Villiers with admiring
deference. A young woman, tall and slight
and pale, dressed in dark colours, rose to her
feet on our entrance, and surveyed Villiers
with curiously brilliant eyes. "Allow me to
introduce you to little Mdlle. Aimée, my best
pensionnaire," said Godefrin; "she is consumed with a desire to play a tragic part, and
I believe she will succeed; ay, and brilliantly!
Perhaps, dear sir," turning to Villiers, "you
will be able to find her a part in your play?"

There was no answer from Villiers. All out
of curl already, he had retired into a corner,

whence he watched us with his suspicious, de-
jected, startled gaze, nervously rolling a cigarette between his fingers.

"Well, let us begin to read!" said I at last,
to break a silence which was becoming em-
barrassing.   We seated ourselves; the poet at
the table, we at random on the seats scattered
about the room.   And the reading began.

I have witnessed many strange scenes in
the course of my life, but never, I think, was
I present at anything so fantastically, irresistibly funny as that sight of Villiers de l'Isle
Adam reading the sheets of his drama to
Godefrin the manager.   At the beginning
things went fairly well.   Villiers seated himself, coughed, moistened his lips in the glass
of water before him, tossed back, with his
usual gesture, the long fair lock which, in spite
of its recent curling, would keep falling over
his eyes, and then, with a searching glance all
round, he opened the manuscript and began :

"Act the first—tableau the first—Swinmore
—the great saloon of Swinmore manor-house,
near Auckland, in the county of Cumberland.
At the rear——"

Here he interrupted himself, rose from his chair, and, with the object of explaining the fittings of the scene to Godefrin, began to jump about the room, knocking over seats, dragging armchairs about, unhooking the arms on a small trophy which hung upon the wall, and accompanying his erratic behaviour with inconsequent sentences and incomprehensible words:

" The balcony of wrought iron-work— night—a moon—stars—there, in the distance, thy silver streak, O sea!—gold enrichments —Ha! ha! ha! they come, the voices! the distant and prophetic voices!—the departing voices!—Ahoy! ahoy! from the boat—here is Ruth, the sad lady of the castle—here is the smiling Mary!—the voices again—the voices approach!—the voices die away!!!—"

Suddenly he perceived the piano, threw himself upon the keyboard, and striking some melancholy chords, he sang in a plaintive voice, "*Adieu, prairie! Adieu, berceau! Adieu, tombeau! Adieu, patrie!*" then, still accompanying himself, recited in sepulchral accents, " Farewell, old house! in which I have never

given happiness, nor enjoyed it! the duty for
which I forsake thee is the most sacred of all
duties in my eyes! God shall be my judge—
yes!—*Adieu, tombeau!*"

Startled and terror-stricken, the correct
frock-coated manager, pale and with com-
pressed lips, had taken refuge in a corner,
whence his wild southern eyes every now and
then shot imploring glances at me. The
actress had buried her head in her hands,
and I could see her pretty shoulders shaking
in a tempest of convulsive laughter. Meanwhile, Villiers, with bristling locks and dis-
trustful eyes, had left the piano, and, standing
with folded arms before Godefrin, he demanded, "Well, sir, have you understood
this mysterious symbolism? Everything,
everything is in that: the parting from the
old country, the uprooting of the young tree
which is to bear the foliage, the fruit, the
perfume of the corrupt Old World in a
newer and purer one. That, the exposition
of the idea of my play, is clearly established,
is it not?" In spite of his astonishment, poor
Godefrin found breath to answer, "Doubtless,

dear sir, your idea is wonderful, but I must humbly admit it has not evolved itself to my intelligence from what I have heard.   May I beg of you to read me your piece quietly, without thinking about the scenery, action, or symbolism ? "

Villiers shrugged his shoulders, his whole physiognomy expressing ineffable scorn and disdain.   He turned to me : " Are you coming?" he said; then taking up his hat and cane, and his manuscript—" Madam ! sir ! I wish you good morning ! " and he moved towards the door.

We surrounded him.   I dragged him back, and made him sit down and listen to me. "Are you stark mad ? " I cried, sternly; "and do you suppose the manager of a theatre is a prophet, who can penetrate the mysteries of a poet's brain, and discover what his ideas are before he condescends to put them into good, plain, intelligible prose ?   Deuce take it !   It is not by pushing about chairs, upsetting furniture, and bawling to the piano, that you will manage to make Godefrin understand your play.   Take my advice; give me your

manuscript" (and I took it out of his hand);
"go and sit down in that farthest corner, and
let me give a complete, ordinary, commonplace reading of your piece."

As I spoke his face darkened; he retired
into a recess, and rolling his eternal cigarette,
his eyes on the ground, he answered in that
hollow voice which he always used when he
desired to personify Doctor Triboulat Bonhomet, "Very good! a family reading! So
be it!" "Bravo!" cried Godefrin, "now we
shall be able to understand what we are about,
and admire in proportion." But I must draw
my story to a close. For two hours I read
without stopping, except to rest for a few
minutes between the acts. If I raised my
eyes, I saw Godefrin listening with an air of
authority, and Villiers lost in distant dreams,
while little Mdlle. Aimée's keen, ardent, concentrated gaze was rivetted on myself. I felt
and understood that she drank in every word
I pronounced, and that every character, as it
shaped itself before her mental vision, became
instinct with life, movement, and suffering;
and when I reached the foot of the last page,

it was her that my eyes instinctively sought. She had risen, quivering with excitement, and hastening to Villiers, she seized both his hands, exclaiming, " Oh, sir, dear sir, I beg you to let me play the part of Mistress Andrews ! " " It is an admirable play," said the impresario, on his side, " and I am ready to make any sacrifice in order to mount such a fine piece of work in a way worthy of its own and its author's merits."

Alas, poor Godefrin ! He little knew the poetic temperament, more capricious than April sunshine, more changeable than the sea. The " Nouveau Monde" was never to be played at Bordeaux. A few months after the scene I have just described, Villiers de l'Isle Adam was back in Paris, and, seduced by the fair promises of Chabrillat, at that time re-organizing the Ambigu, he withdrew his piece from the director of the Bordeaux theatre, to confide it to this suddenly-arisen literary Barnum. It is greatly to be regretted that Bordeaux should not have had the first per-formance of this fine play. I am convinced that Villiers' work would there have achieved the enthusiastic success which it merits, and everyone will agree with me that no Parisian stage could have furnished an artist more capable of interpreting the gloomy *rôle* of the heroine than little Mdlle. Aimée, M. Godefrin's *pensionnaire;* for Madame Aimée Tessandier, of the Comédie Française, is now, and justly, considered one of our finest and most gifted tragic actresses, and Godefrin was a true prophet when he predicted that her success would be great.

Little Mdlle. Aimée of those bygone days! If chance should bring these lines before your eyes, you may perhaps forget for a moment your recent glories in the house of Molière, and give a thought to the distant past! That part of Mistress Andrews, madame, was a very beautiful creation, and one which might well inspire such an artistic individuality as yours. It might have marked an important stage in your triumphal march ; it might, even now, did you choose to take it back and play it to the life, become the fairest pearl in your diadem as a tragic actress !

CHAPTER IX.

Restful days—The real Villiers—Villiers and the fair sex—Talks about bygone days—Charles Baudelaire—His true nature—His strange home-life—Jeanne Duval—Edgar Poe—Richard Wagner—"Axël"—The Cabala and the occult sciences—Villiers' religious sentiments—Quotations—"L'Eve Future."

THOSE days spent with my friend far from the cares and noise of city life, have remained with me as one of my pleasantest memories. For us they were days of delicious and beneficial repose. In that quiet sunny southern spot where we spent some weeks together, the mantle of bitter scorn and scepticism in which he wrapped himself on the boulevards seemed to drop from his shoulders. I penetrated far into his inner nature, and he allowed me to

perceive the ideal and beautiful personality
which he so jealously concealed in the depths
of his soul.   Thus I came to know at last a
Villiers de l'Isle Adam but little resembling
the one who used to delight the nightly
frequenters of the *brasseries* at Montmartre
by his wit, his strange imaginings, and his
disconnected manner of life.   This was the real
man, the dreamer, the philosopher, the poet,
the true lover, incarnated in the superhuman
character of Axël, and concealed beneath the
cloak of irony in which all his work is en-
folded.

On those cloudless balmy nights at Bordeaux, as we wandered in close converse along
the banks of the great river, under the graceful
arches of the pine-trees, through which the
pale and mysterious moonbeams slanted,
while above us rose the hill-slopes covered
with the heavy purple and golden bunches of
the ripening grapes, he would go back over
his past life, and would recount to me and to
himself his intellectual and sentimental history.   Did woman play a great part in the
poet's life?   I think so, though he had few

adventures and fewer passionate attachments.
But, like that much misunderstood personage,
Don Juan, Villiers was continually seeking
that divine emotion which he never felt but
once, and that in his early youth, during the
short existence of that first and purest love of
which the green Breton fields were the cradle,
the setting, and the grave. /If he chanced to
catch sight of one of those celestial faces
which make one believe that angels may
come down to earth, he would fall in love
with his own ideal. But as soon as he approached a woman more closely, his pitiless
spirit of analysis laid bare all the moral ugli-
nesses and littlenesses veiled by her physical
beauty. The angel disappeared, and brutal
reality clipped the wings of his dream. After
a disappointment of this sort, he would throw
himself with a sort of frenzy into the wildest
orgies of midnight debauchery. At such times
his sarcasms about love and women burnt like
a redhot iron, but beneath all his imprecations
one felt that there lay the despair of a man
who has held for one short moment the key of
Eden, and from whom it has been snatched

before he could open the sacred portal. Happily his art, his love for it, and his consciousness of his own genius, consoled him for his many mortifications.

He loved, in these intimate and often retrospective conversations, to go back over the first happy years of his residence in Paris, to his friendly relations with my father, and above all to Charles Baudelaire, whose memory haunted him like a ghost. They had made acquaintance at the office of the " Revue Fantaisiste," whither, from time to time, the author of the "Fleurs du Mal" would bring some of his original and ex-quisitely-polished "Petits Poèmes en Prose." Baudelaire and Villiers had too much in common not to be quickly drawn together. From the date of their first meeting they were frequently in each other's company, and Villiers was one of the few friends who were present at the poet's terrible death. For my own part, while greatly admiring Baudelaire as a poetical craftsman, I did not like his character as an individual. From all I had heard (for I never knew him personally), he seemed to me to be wanting in sincerity, and to be eternally posing, not only before the public, but before the little circle over which he habitually presided.

Villiers would leap with rage if I expressed this in his presence. He declared that I swam in a sea of stupid prejudice; that what I took for affectation in Baudelaire was really the essence of his extraordinary nature ; that he could not be nor behave otherwise. And he would try to explain this strange, terribly complicated character to me, diabolical as it was in some ways, exquisitely good in others. Would that my impotent pen could reproduce the fire, the eagerness, and the brilliancy of Villiers' speeches in defence of his departed friend! Baudelaire had condescended to explain and analyze himself, to lay bare his heart, as he expressed it, before this priviledged associate. "In his youth," said Villiers, "he halted between two ambitions. To be the greatest actor in the world, or else to be—the Pope." Although he had shouldered a musket and worn the workman's blouse in 1848, he gave himself out as a Catholic and a

supporter of constituted authority. "A Catholic possessed by a devil," Villiers would add,
"and a supporter of authority who admitted
none but his own, and that of his vices, which
he cherished as works of art, and of which he
was inordinately proud."   Nothing could have
been more strikingly curious than the description given by the author of "Axël" of the
poet's home-life.   He lived near Neuilly, in
an apartment with large high rooms, full of
oddly-shaped furniture, Chinese monsters,
Indian idols, fantastic and generally frightful
carvings of animals, the walls of which were
hung with dark and revolting pictures of the
Spanish School, mutilations, executions, and
torture scenes, painted by the horror-loving
Ribeira and his pupils.   In the midst of this
nightmare scene Baudelaire moved slowly
about, cold, silent, and pale, himself half-
frightened, like one who walks through a
hideous dream.   And as mistress of this
strange dwelling, there was a creature stranger
still—a coloured girl, almost a negress, named
Jeanne Duval, always shivering, and wrapped
in gaudy silks, past her youth, thin, cringing,

and without any charm but that of her glowing
eyes.   Violent, bad-tempered, untruthful, un-
faithful, greedy, intemperate, and depraved,
she died a drunkard's death in the Maison
Dubois, idolized and petted to her last gasp
by Baudelaire, who loved her deeply, I suppose for the sake of her many perversities.

It was to Charles Baudelaire that Villiers
owed one of his greatest artistic enjoyments,
his acquaintance with the works of Edgar Poe.
He was a very bad English scholar, and
without his friend's wonderful translations,
and his enthusiastic talk on the subject of the
great American story-teller, he would never,
probably, have made acquaintance with the
"Strange Tales," nor with that wonderful
poem, "The Raven," which he used to recite
in such a striking manner.   And it was the
will of fate that he should owe yet more to
Baudelaire.   It was in his house that he saw
for the first time the only human genius before
whom he ever completely and unreservedly
bowed down, Richard Wagner.   This meeting,
the most important event, according to Villiers,
in his intellectual life, took place in the month of

May, 1861. The wizard of music had called to thank Baudelaire for a fine, and, for those days, very courageous study of himself and his work, published in the " Revue Européenne," and entitled " Richard Wagner and Tannhäuser." This was the beginning of one of those beautiful and noble artistic friendships of which, alas! so few examples exist, and the bond of which was only to be severed by death. In a future chapter of these recollections, I shall speak more fully, as is fitting, of the intimacy between these two highly-gifted beings, so well formed for mutual understanding, the creator of Elsa and the creator of Axël.

Already, at the time of his sojourn in the south of France, Villiers was at work on that great philosophical drama of " Axël," which only appeared after he was dead.

One of the most wonderful scenes in the work (Part II., " Le Monde Tragique," scene 8), was entirely written at Bordeaux.

For the purposes of this play Villiers had profoundly studied the Cabala and the occult sciences, both past and present. Yet his mind was too powerful and too analytical to be profoundly smitten by such theories.   He merely saw in them a phase of the philoso-phical evolution of centuries, and he also found in them dramatic elements of the highest order.   But I venture to assert, from what I have known of him, that it would be a mistake to reckon the author of the "Nouveau Monde" among contemporary cabalists.

His ideal soared further and higher far than the magic art cultivated so assiduously, and not altogether unremuneratively, by that long-haired young sar, Joséphin Péladan. Though the occult sciences may overwhelm and infatuate the intelligence of Péladan at the close of this century, and Rohan at the dawn of the Revolution, to such vigorous geniuses as Goethe in Germany and Villiers de l'Isle Adam in France they are but a step to be boldly taken in the approach towards divine truth.

And I should like to say here, to the honour of the great writer whose work and character have been so much misunderstood, that Villiers de l'Isle Adam was all his life a convinced and fervent Roman Catholic.   The study of the

philosophy of all times and every country, the
study of the human mind, and the study of
nature, all only strengthened his faith. He
firmly believed that God was good, and that
the Devil was wicked, in Heaven, in Purgatory,
in Hell. Through all those hours of physical
agony and moral suffering which he endured
before his soul escaped to Paradise, he found
the source of all his hope and all his consolation in prayer. His life, indeed, like the lives
of most great artists, was full of faults and
failures, but whenever he had a chance of
fighting the good fight in the cause of religion and of our divine ideal, he did it with a
fervour and an enthusiasm which proved the
sincerity of his convictions. And doubtless
God will count that to him for righteous-
ness.

"One of the most deeply-rooted feelings in
Villiers' soul," wrote M. G. Guiches, very
truly, the day after the poet's death ("Figaro,"
August 18, 1889), "was the strong, honest,
tender, religious sentiment which would make
his eyes fill with tears whenever the divine
mysteries were spoken of in his presence.

Neither the promiscuous café life, throughout
which he always preserved his haughty independence of heart and mind, nor his copious
and inventive flow of banter, ever touched
with the faintest stain the royal ermine of his
faith.   On those loose sheets on which, like
Baudelaire, he was in the habit of noting
down his thoughts, side by side with prosaic
memoranda of daily life, and naïve resolutions,
such as 'not to smoke so much,' phrases like
the following occur : 'It is a sin to mourn for
a dead child.   It has entered into its glory.'
Among these fragments, too, are touching
litanies to the Virgin : 'Mother of the good
God! O thou, my Mother! thou who
intercedest, sure that thou shalt be heard!
Thou who standest on Calvary! Thou who
canst pardon! Heel that crushest the serpent! Whiteness of the eternal dawn! Glory
of human tears! Light of the eastern star!
Thou soul of chastity! Thou resignation of
the poor!' etc., etc., etc.

   "To an author who told him the atro-
ciously cynical title of his lately-published
book, he answered boldly: 'Such things

should never be written. Those are words that will come back to you on your death-bed.'"

As I am in a vein of quotation, I will cite one more charming anecdote on the same subject, related in the "Revue Blanc" by M. Henri Laujol, one of Villiers' earliest comrades.

"I remember," he says, "receiving a visit from Villiers one day, while I was reading Hœckel's 'History of the Creation.' I can see him now, turning over the leaves, looking at the woodcuts, and weighing the book in his hand, with much pantomimic alarm. He asked how much that grand book had cost, and I told him the price, somewhere about ten francs. 'The catechism costs only two sous!' was his reply. It was a regular country parson's remark. But Villiers was so delighted at having made it that he spent his whole afternoon repeating it to me, droning it out in every sort of key, now falsetto, now bass, and then again in a Tyrolese jodel; interrupting himself, now and then, to laugh at the top of his voice. I could get nothing else out of him the whole of that day."

But I must turn from our bygone talks to register here an incident of his life on the boulevards, which he related to me one evening, and which was to give birth to that famous novel, "L'Eve Future," which appeared long afterwards at Brunhoff's, with this motto attached to it : "*Transitoriis quære æterna.*"

CHAPTER X.

A metamorphosis—An ambitious pastry-cook—Appearance
of the newspaper, "La Croix et l'Epée"—Its political,
artistic, and literary programme—Lord E—— W——
—His strange suicide—The wax figure—A nocturnal
conversation—The American engineer and his
master, Edison—First conception of "L'Eve Future"
—Villiers de l'Isle Adam and Thomas Alva Edison.

NOT long before the famous Lockroy
lawsuit, Villiers de l'Isle Adam, for
the first time in his life, had found
himself in a regularly established
position. He had given the frequenters of
the boulevards and of the newspaper offices
the unwonted spectacle of a Villiers in brand-
new clothes and a brilliantly smart silk hat—
a Villiers with a grave face and a well-filled
pocket-book, whose fingers rattled keys and
five-franc pieces together in his pockets—a

Villiers, in fine, who breakfasted at the Café Riche, and had his table every night at Brébant's (that restaurant so dear to literary men), in the celebrated first-floor room so graphically described in the journals of the De Goncourt. The reason of this ephemeral change in the poet's life is worthy of a place in the "Arabian Nights." A retired confectioner, devoured by political and literary ambition, and convinced, doubtless, that his success in making fancy biscuits gave him a right to put his fingers into the great political pie, desired to found a newspaper to be the organ of his opinions. This, in itself, is a very ordinary fact, not particularly worthy of note. Many an ambitious vulgarian is not content without a newspaper slavishly devoted to his interests. But this pastry-cook, who shall be nameless, became absolutely heroic, and undoubtedly worthy to be mentioned to posterity when, out of all the starving writers who trod the cruel and horrible Paris pavements, he chose that unmerciful scoffer, Villiers de l'Isle Adam, as his representative and *alter ego*.

A play or a story might be written about the ups and downs of the astounding newspaper which was the outcome of this strange union.   I have only time to throw some hasty touches on the canvas.

Villiers was chief editor, reporter, critic, and article-writer at one and the same time.   The confectioner was director, manager, and cashier. He gave the poet five hundred francs a month, and left him absolutely free to express his own political, artistic, and literary opinions, exacting two things only : firstly, that " his newspaper " should mention him, individually, every day ; and secondly, that " his newspaper " should make a stir in the capital.   His desire was more than gratified !

" La Croix et l'Epée," the Cross and Sword (high-sounding title !), claimed, in matters of religion, the right of every soldier to swear round oaths and go to mass ; politically, it supported the claim of the Naundorffs to the throne of France ; artistically, it put the symbolist painters above Raphael ; poetically, it proclaimed Stéphane Mallarmé the prince of rhyme, and defended the School of the Incom-

prehensibles; and musically, it was belligerently
and exclusively Wagnerian. At the end of
six months the newspaper disappeared, the
confectioner went back to his province, and
Villiers found himself back on the boulevards,
poorer than ever in pocket, but rich still in
splendid hopes, and answering the hypo-
critical condolences of his fellow-journalists
with his usual phrase, "Yes, yes! Many
thanks! But all is not lost! Next winter, we
shall see!"

It was during this period of relative prosperity that he caught a glimpse of the individual who gave him the first idea for his
novel, "L'Eve Future."

One evening he saw coming into Brébant's,
arm-in-arm with one of the attachés of the
British Embassy, a young Englishman whose
singular face aroused his imagination.

"He was both handsome and sad-looking,"
Villiers used to tell me, in his enthusiastic
way, "and I saw at once in the expression of
his eyes that grave and scornful look of
melancholy which always betokens a hidden
despair."

This young man's name (I only give the
initials) was Lord E—— W——.   His tragic
end attracted attention in Paris for some time.
He destroyed himself, very deliberately, some
days after Villiers met him.   Stretched beside
him, in a magnificent dress, bespattered with
his blood, was found an admirably-made lay
figure, representing a young woman, whose
waxen face, modelled by a great artist, was
the portrait of a young lady well known in
London for her brilliant beauty, and who had
been engaged to be married to the eccentric
young nobleman.

Was this suicide merely the result of one
of those strange hereditary manias which
afflict some families of the English aristo-
cracy?   Or was the mysterious catastrophe
of some dramatic and passionate love affair
to be read in the presence of the wonderful
doll on the young man's deathbed?   The
young attaché inclined to this latter opinion.
According to his view, Lord E—— W——
had been the victim of an extraordinary
fatality.   He adored the physical loveliness
of the young girl; he was perpetually haunted

M

by her magnificent beauty; but he held her mind and soul, and everything in her that was not material, in the deepest abhorrence. Hence arose the slowly-developed madness which ended in his death.

These things were related one night at the restaurant, before Villiers and a small circle of *habitués*. An American engineer—an electrician, as they call them over there—rose from his seat, and quietly said, " I am sorry your friend did not apply to me; I might have cured him." "You! how?" "How! Great Scott! I would have given his doll life, soul, movement, love!" The assembled company, being sceptical as to miracles, burst out laughing, all but Villiers, who seemed to be absorbed in rolling his cigarette. " You may laugh, stranger," said the American gravely, as he picked up his hat and stick, "but the time will come when my great master, Edison, will teach you that electricity is an almighty power," and with that he went out.

These facts and this nocturnal conversation gave birth to " L'Eve Future," one of the most original works of this end of the century.

Those who have perused this masterpiece of eloquent raillery, by the poet who, to use M. Henri Laujol's happy expression, "had vowed a monkish hatred against modern science, that handmaid of utilitarianism," will doubtless recollect that the general notion and argument of the story follow almost identically the facts I have just related.   But Villiers was not one of those half-artists who are satisfied with their first idea, and work it out the moment chance has presented it to their brain.   It was only after revolving it in his mind, pondering and brooding over it, that he began to write his novel, the first wonderful pages of which, with their description of Menloe Park and its terrifying proprietor, Thomas Alva Edison, he read to me in 1879.

When the great inventor himself came to Paris in 1889 to see our exhibition, somebody sent him De l'Isle Adam's book.   He read it through without putting it down, and said to one of his intimates, "That man is greater than I.   I can only invent.   He creates!"   He desired to make the author's acquaintance, but, alas! poor Villiers, already stricken by the fell disease of which he died, could not respond to Edison's invitation. This is deeply to be regretted. Can anything more curious and more interesting be imagined than a conversation between the progenitor of Dr. Triboulat Bonhomet and the father of the phonograph?

Soon after he had related the curious origin of his contemplated work to me, my eccentric friend suddenly disappeared from my sight.

CHAPTER XI.

Villiers' absent-mindedness—His terrible carelessness—
His departure from Bordeaux—Godefrin's despair—
A year later—Bohemian poverty—A justification—
Want of money—Villiers' difficulties—His pride—
His artistic conscientiousness—Drumont's book—
Villiers and the young Jew—A good answer—Villiers'
manner of life—His midnight wanderings—His dis-
·like of daylight—Villiers and Anatole France.

MOST disconcerting thing about
Villiers, which used to exasperate
his best friends till his dying day,
was his perpetual absent-minded-
ness, which led him to forget the most important appointments, to break off, for long
months on end, his most intimate daily
relations, and only occasionally to fulfil the
engagements he might make with editors of
reviews or publishers. The uncertainty of
his movements kept one continually on the

alert; you could never tell when he would come or when he would go. I have described his sudden apparition in my house at Bordeaux. His departure was just as unexpected. We had talked the whole night long; at early dawn I went to get a little rest, and when I rose it was already late. I inquired after Villiers; he had gone out, and hours passed without his return. In vain I sought him. Without beat of drum he had disappeared, melted away like a shadow.

A few days after I met Godefrin with a long face. He had just received a letter from the inconstant writer, dated from Paris, demanding the immediate return of the manuscript of the "Nouveau Monde." His conversation was one flood of recriminations. For my own part, inured long since as I was to the poet's offhand ways, I was only half-surprised, and I did my best to console the unhappy director, whom I have not had the good fortune to meet since that interview.

Towards me Villiers preserved an unbroken silence. Indeed, I might have thought him dead, and myself forgotten, if the post had not brought me packets containing articles, tales, or fanciful conceits of his, cut out of newspapers and magazines, and which, addressed as they were by his own hand, proved that he was not "the late De l'Isle Adam," and that I still lived in his memory.

It was difficult, after all was said and done, to bear him a grudge because of his exasperating carelessness, for when you next met him, after a disappearance of five or six months, he would address you as if he had only left you the night before.   If you reproached him, he would gaze at you with an innocent and puzzled air, seemingly quite unconscious of his sin ; and then he had such a particular way of exclaiming, "What! I did that! oh, come, come! impossible! you must be chaffing me!" that nobody could keep their countenance nor their bad temper long.   Personally I was not to see him for two years.   Alas! when we met again in Paris in 1879, I saw that poverty was slowly accomplishing its destructive work.   Never had the Bohemian life which he so courageously accepted, seemed more utterly dreary. He needed all his power of hopefulness to

endure it.   But though his heart was as stout,
his imagination as brilliant, his mind as active
as ever, the bodily frame was beginning to tire
and its machinery to break down, thanks to
bad food, want of care, and the late hours
and noxious tobacco-laden air of tavern life.
Living as I did in Paris the whole of that year,
I contrived to withdraw him a little from the
infernal round which was destroying his life.
But I never deceived myself.   I felt it was
only a respite, and that he would always have
a longing for that eccentric and feverish existence which devoured him body and soul and
hastened his end.

This year of grace 1879 was the last we
spent together, and it was the time of our
closest intimacy. Before reviving some memories of it, I desire to defend Villiers against an
unjust accusation, which is frequently brought
against him. He has been accused, both in life
and after death, of being a dissipated tavern-
bird, a lover of low company. It has been
asserted that his want of success arose principally from his own bad conduct, his want of
moral sense, his indolence, and the doubtful

company he frequented.   To those who only knew him casually these accusations bear an appearance of truth fatal to the poet's good name.   But we who were acquainted with his inner life, and have watched him through the hard trials of his laborious existence, know how little he deserved the reproaches of these wiseacres. We knew the nobility of his nature, the innate delicacy of his tastes, his passion for work, his scorn of material enjoyments. And we know how, little by little, this gifted being was driven by evil fortune to live in an atmosphere unworthy of him, and how, too, little by little, and after many a revolt, he grew accustomed to it.

May I be permitted, then, within the space of a few lines, to attempt the justification of the slipshod and Bohemian manner of life of Villiers de l'Isle Adam.   It will give me an opportunity of showing the original and complex character of the artist in a new light.

The faithful autobiography of a writer living in Paris during the last twenty years, without any other means of support than his own talents, would be a gloomier and a sadder

book than Dante's " Inferno." But it would
likewise be a healthy and instructive one, a
sort of warning beacon which should save
many a young and promising life from ruin,
shame, and death. Though there are some
indomitable natures which rise higher and
gain in strength through the struggle with
misfortune, there are many more, and highly
gifted ones too, which are lowered and
crushed down by despicable cares, grinding
poverty, and anxiety concerning the earning
of daily bread. True as it may be that
energy, moral strength, and artistic conviction
form a solid suit of armour, yet I hold that the
thinnest silver cuirass is more useful for win-
ning the final victory. And that which hin-
dered Villiers from climbing to the highest
eminence was above all things his want of
money.

This condition of penury must have been
all the more prejudicial and painful to him,
because the *début* of his career was so successful as to be almost an apotheosis.

Excessively proud, and with a lively sentiment for the illustrious name he bore, he

would never, when poverty came upon him, undertake any of those lucrative, if ignoble jobs, which in these days are always to be had about the literary world. He carried his respect for his calling as far as his respect for his ancestry, and no matter how pressing his need was, he would never send a hastily-finished page, nor even sentence, to the printer. He read and re-read everything, first low, then loud, and finally, when the whole was weeded and corrected, he would declaim it in that clear sonorous voice which he always used when reciting his own writings. According to him, the worst crime a writer can commit is to sell himself. And in this connection I will record an authenticated anecdote which ends with a remark by the author of "L'Eve Future" which almost touches the sublime.

Immediately after the appearance of "La France Juive," the Jewish community in Paris looked about for a writer equal to the task of returning the murderous knockdown blows of the terrible Drumont. Somebody suggested Villiers de l'Isle Adam. A noble

name, a brilliant talent, and in straits of
poverty—probably to be had very cheap! A
nice little glossy well-combed Jew, who then
looked, perhaps still looks, after the censor-
ship in the back office of a fashionable publisher, was sent to call upon him. Villiers,
struggling with the direst poverty, often
without half a franc in his pocket, was living
in a big, bare, dark, cold room, somewhere
on the heights of Montmartre, where he
still possessed an old easy-chair, a ricketty
table, and a poor asthmatic piano, which the
bailiffs had despised. Here the young Jew
found the last descendant of the Grand Master of the Order of St. John of Jerusalem.
Unctuously servile, and with an exaggerated
show of respect, the messenger of the syna-
gogue explained its desire, concluding by
saying that there could be no bargaining
with a writer of such distinction, and that the
Comte Villiers de l'Isle Adam had only to
name his own price. Then he waited in
silence for the answer of Villiers, who had
listened without interrupting, rolling a cigarette in his white fingers, his absent glance half

hidden by the thick lock that fell over his
brow.   When his interlocutor had ceased
speaking, he raised his head, and fixing on
him his clear blue eyes, filled now with
sudden flame, he answered in a ringing
voice, " My price, sir ? It has not altered
since the days of our Saviour! Thirty pieces
of silver!"   Then, rising and wrapping
around him his tattered old dressing-gown,
he pointed to the door with a gesture that
the illustrious marshal, his ancestor, might
have envied, and added, " Begone, sir !"

But I have wandered from my subject.
I was saying that poverty had been a hard
stepmother to Villiers de l'Isle Adam, forcing
him from his youth up to shape his life to
the Bohemian habits of a vagabond Parisian
life, and to such habits he gradually became
accustomed.   Serious and well-established
people, as well as self-important and overfed
middle-class folk, used to reproach him bit-
terly with the carelessness of his existence,
with his slipshod behaviour, above all, with
his assiduous frequentation of those nocturnal
places of entertainment, which, under the

name of wine-shops, *brasseries*, and artists' taverns, swarm between the Faubourg Montmartre and the Boulevard de Clichy. Yet how many good excuses there were for this so-called life of idleness and debauchery!

If Villiers, without being rich, had possessed a few pounds a year, if he could have made for himself, somewhere in the formidable city, ever so small a corner where he might have dreamed his brilliant beautiful dreams, and written, and thought, without anxiety concerning his daily pittance,—I, who was his friend, will affirm that the witty and eloquent frequenters of the "Chat Noir" and the "Rat Mort" would have known him less, and, what is more to the purpose, less intimately. But driven by dire necessity to pitch his tent in some empty lodging or dreary hotel room, he had such a horror, aristocratic being, dainty poet, charming artist as he was, of the hideous dwellings into which his evil fate had penned him, that he fled from them, preferring to make all Paris his home, and to say, in the words of Bruant's working man, " T'es dans la rue,

va, t'es chez toi!"—"You're in the gutter?
then you are at home!"

It was walking the pavements, on the
terraces of cafés, and with his elbow on the
stained tavern tables, that he imagined, discussed, and partly wrote, some of his finest
works. Every imaginative being, moreover,
wants some nervous excitement to quicken
his brain process, and Villiers more especially
was the victim of this need. He could not
evolve his ideas and present them clearly
to his own mind without discussion, and
therefore without somebody to discuss them
with. If prosperity had been granted to him,
he might have found all this in artistic circles,
at his own fireside, in friendly gatherings,
perhaps in the drawing-room of some woman
of fashion. Poor as he was, and driven into
Bohemian life, he had to fall back on his
wild nocturnal habits, and on the hubbub
of the tavern, where ideas and words meet
and clash noisily through clouds of tobacco
smoke, amidst the rattle of glasses and the
noisy laughter of loose women.

I owe it, however, to truth to say that

Villiers' love of late hours was not altogether the result of circumstances. He was essentially a night-bird. He hated the daylight, and always called the sun a hideous planet, which, he declared, lighted nature up badly, and spoiled her beauty. Even in his best days, he never became quite himself until his kindly little friends the stars blinked down at him out of the sky.

The brilliant critic of the "Temps," M. Anatole France, tells us, in a kindly sketch dedicated to the memory of De l'Isle Adam, that, being in want of exact information concerning the poet's ancestors for some literary work on which he was engaged, he went one day to look him up at his lodgings at Montmartre. He was received smilingly, but when he announced the object of his visit, the master of the house looked perplexed, doubtful, and troubled. He began to stammer, and at last, almost in tears, he exclaimed : " How can you expect me to talk to you about my ancestors, the illustrious grand master and the famous marshal, in bright sunshine like this, at ten o'clock in the morning ? " He really was in utter dismay, and the witty critic had to exert himself to the utmost to restore him to his equanimity and obtain the necessary information from him.

CHAPTER XII.

IN 1879 Villiers inhabited a room in a furnished hotel in the Rue des Martyrs, nearly at the corner of the Rue Clauzel. Chance had made us neighbours, for I was living at the corner of the Rue Rochechouart and the Rue de Maubeuge, at the very top of an enormous house let out in flats, and from my balcony I could see all over Paris. As to the poet's room, it was just as commonplace as might have been expected in a tenth-rate furnished lodging-house. A mahogany bed, chair, and chest of drawers, an imitation Wilton carpet, and the inevitable wardrobe with a looking-glass in it.   Should this last happen to gape open, one perceived on every shelf, not linen, nor clothes of any description, but piles of manuscript, books, newspapers, and magazines.

The extreme indifference of the great writer to the material comforts of life greatly assisted him in bearing the pangs of poverty. I never knew him take thought for the morrow, in the literal sense of the term, though he thought and talked a great deal about the future in general.   But he never troubled his head as to whether he had a shirt to his back ; and had it not been for the care of some devoted friends, I really believe he would have ended by going out-of-doors half-dressed, or by spending several months in bed for want of clothes.   Luckily, a sort of earthly providence seemed to watch over him, and supply his most pressing needs. One of his best loved and most faithful friends, Léon Dierx, lived in the same house, and looked after him without seeming to do so, for Villiers was as touchy as he was careless.

But, above all others, there was a worthy
woman, a retired midwife, who had attached
herself to the poet with a canine devotion
which used to bring the tears to my eyes. The
jests, the snubbing, even the furies of her
idol, could not dishearten her. She treated
him with a delicate tenderness which the
most passionately devoted mistress might have
envied. The great writer, with the Bohemian
indifference of the man who owns nothing,
used, when he came in at dawn, worn out
with holding forth and discussing, to leave
his door unlocked, and the key in it. This
excellent soul would seize her opportunity,
come in on tiptoe, take his poor, stained,
shabby garments, mend them as best she
could, and then restore them to their place.
Often she would bring a clean shirt, and lay
it on the foot of the bed. When Villiers took
it into his head to get up and go out, about
the time the gas was being lighted in the
streets, he would put on the first thing that
came under his hand, without ever noticing
the changes in and additions to his wardrobe
made by this admirable woman, whom we

had nicknamed " La Dévouée," " the devoted
one."   When I became the poet's neighbour,
I often made use of her.   She would put
coats and trousers of mine beside him while
he slept ; and I often had a struggle to keep
my countenance when I saw my friend dressed
up in my cast-off clothes, which used to give
him a most peculiar appearance, for while I
was long and thin, he was short and broad.
But he went on unmoved, and never suspected
anything.

The waiter of the hotel had also been
coached.   He used to enter Villiers' room,
every day towards noon, carrying a large
bowl of soup, into which a penny roll had
been cut up.   Should the poet be asleep, he
took care not to rouse him.   If Villiers was
awake, he would call out threateningly,
" What's that ? "   " Breakfast, sir ! " said the
waiter, and hastily putting the bowl down,
he departed.   Mechanically Villiers would
swallow bread and soup, and think no more
of the almost daily recurring incident.   He
never had any other meal before his evening one.

I got into the habit of going to see him
between three and four o'clock in the afternoons.   I generally found him sitting up in
bed, supported by several pillows, hard at work,
and only stopping his writing to roll a cigarette, which, as often as not, he did not light.
Lying on the eiderdown quilt, which covered
his knees, was a pouchful of his favourite
Maryland tobacco, books of cigarette papers,
and piles of sheets covered with his fine and
delicately-formed handwriting.   He never
wrote with anything but pencil, which made
the compositors' work very difficult, especially
as in reading his work over he would generally alter one word out of five.

As soon as he saw me (sometimes I stood
in front of him for ten minutes before he was
aware of my presence, so completely did his
work absorb him), he would start, and exclaim,
" What, is that you, cousin? What o'clock
is it? The window, the window!" and before
I could do anything to stop him, he would
jump out of bed, and, regardless of weather or
temperature, throw the window wide open.
Then he would get back into bed, put his

hand through his heavy forelock, look at me
in a confused sort of way, and end by bursting out laughing.   These antics usually had
the result of sending tobacco, cigarettes, and
sheets of paper flying across the room, and, if
there was any wind, whirling round the table.
I used to rush to the rescue of the precious
prose, and when I had collected and put the
scattered manuscript in order as well as I
could, I would sit down in the only armchair,
and our talks would begin.   At last, towards
six o'clock, and by dint of persecution, I contrived to drag him from between the sheets,
and out we went into the streets.

The street! Ah! when one walked it arm-in-
arm with Villiers, it was no longer a commonplace and more or less symmetrical assemblage
of paving-stones, asphalte side-walks, road-
ways, shops, and houses.   It became a strange
entity, with a million different living existences
—a hybrid, complex, contradictory being, by
turns mysterious, terrible, cynical, innocent,
cruel, loving, tragic, or grotesque.   By dint
of treading it for so many years, he had taken
root in it, and was, so to speak, one of the

strangest products, the most striking types, of
that world, at once so great and so limited, in
which certain figures stand out with such
clearness from the moving mass, that, once
seen, they can never be forgotten.   Amongst
those physiognomies which seem to form an
integral part of the street crowd, and which
one misses there when death removes them,
some are dramatic, some comic, some hideous.
Some are sad, some poetic, others mad ; but
all attract your attention, and even obtrude
themselves on your notice, by some personal
originality of appearance.   And in no case
more so than in that of Villiers de l'Isle Adam,
with his supple and yet uncertain gait, his
immeasurable scorn of the laws of fashion, and
that sleep-walking look which the cruel and
much dreaded irony of his speech and laughter
belied.   He knew all the secrets, all the hidden
sores, all the grandeur, of the merciless streets
of Paris.   In the course of our perambula-
tions together, he would point out to me
houses of whose secret dramas, comedies, or
idylls, he knew every detail.   He would explain, with that sort of stammer which added

to the charm of his talk, that the exterior
of houses generally matched their interior
history; that there were murderous ones,
broken-hearted ones, gay ones; that some
were passionate, some sepulchral, some volup-
tuous, ay, and some haunted even.   For he
averred, and quoted many a strange story in
support of his opinion, that there were more
haunted houses in Paris than in any other
town in Europe.   Several of them he had
inhabited himself.   And the recent events in
the house on the Quai Voltaire would have
filled him with delight.   I make no doubt
whatever he would have liked to live there.

But it was especially when we reached the
Boulevard Montmartre "à l'heure de l'absinthe," that Villiers became my most invaluable guide and cicerone.   All that population
of charlatans which swarms before the cafés,
money-lenders, money-getters, and rogues—
sham litterateurs and sham artists—jour-
nalists, venal, if not already bought, scandal-
mongers, masters in the art of blackmail,
stealers of other men's ideas, well-dressed
blackguards, elegantly apparelled demi-mon-

daines, swindlers, *rastaquouères*, he unmasked
them all in short, sharp, vengeful sentences,
burning with implacable scorn.   And in the
very bitterness of his satire, one felt how
these beasts of prey must have devoured his
flesh and his substance.   They meanwhile
pretended to respect, while hating and fearing
him.   They dreaded those terrible sarcasms,
which the next day's papers would noise
abroad, as the galley-slave dreads the brand-
ing iron.   So they bowed themselves down
before him, and as soon as he was past they
stabbed him in the back.

After these walks, Villiers often came and
shared the simple dinner which my Breton
cook used to prepare for me ; and this made
a change for him from the indescribable and
poisonous eating-house stews on which he
was in the habit of feeding.

There were two things besides the fact of
our friendship which had the precious gift of
retaining Villiers in my house during the
evening hours : my balcony, and an excellent
piano by Pleyel, which was the chief adorn-
ment of the little sitting-room.

On soft clear nights we used to spend much of our time leaning over the balcony, smoking almost silently, and letting our dreamy thoughts, grave or gay, wander across the great tumultuous-looking sea of roofs, whose dark, motionless waves seemed to lose themselves in the mists of the horizon. Now and then Villiers would draw himself up, erect and very pale, and stretching out his white hand, as though to claim the attention of the night, he would recite in a ringing voice some passage out of whatever work he might be engaged upon. His memory was so good that he knew by heart almost everything he had ever written. In such surroundings the effect was profoundly impressive. High over our heads the twinkling stars; at our feet the huge city, its continuous roar rising towards us; while from the lips of the poet the harmoniously balanced periods fell in even, eloquent flow, clear, sonorous, and strangely melodious. He would work himself up at the sound of his own voice, and, his eyes fixed in a sort of ecstasy and his gestures raised to God, he seemed no longer

to belong to earth.   And I listened, dumb
with admiration.   And when at last he
ceased to speak, it seemed to me that a lamp
had suddenly gone out, and that the world
was darkened around me.   Villiers thus
recited to me all the finest passages of "L'Eve
Future," and I vividly remember the state
of wild delight into which we were both put
by the chapter headed "The Puppet addresses
the Night."[1]   We would re-enter the drawing-
room, and Villiers, still shivering with the
excitement of inspiration, would rush to the
piano, and, striking some powerful chords,
would begin with the full strength of his
voice the magnificent choral invocation in
the first act of " Lohengrin "—" *O Dieu du
Ciel en qui j'ai foi !* "

If Villiers had applied himself to music,
instead of choosing literature as his profession,
I believe he might have been as remarkable
and original a composer as he was a writer.
Music is, of all the arts, the one which
requires the greatest number of innate and,

---

[1] In the final edition this chapter bears the title
"God."

so to speak, instinctive qualities, and these natural gifts he possessed to an extraordinary degree. From his earliest youth he had a feeling for rhythm and time, a correctness of ear, and a musical memory, which astonished his teachers. Yet he was never a good pupil, because in this, as in everything else, he loathed routine, and would not submit to a humdrum daily task. But, though he journeyed into the domain of literature, his qualities as a gifted musician followed him thither, and his very prose is musical.

In the course of his life he composed or improvised a goodly number of strange melodies, songs, *melopœia*, which unfortunately have never been collected. The best known, which all his friends have heard him sing, and to which I have already referred, interprets that wonderful poem by Charles Baudelaire :

> Nous aurons des lits pleins d'odeurs légères,
> Des divans profonds comme des tombeaux.

> Our beds shall be scented with sweetest perfume,
> Our divans be as cool and as dark as the tomb.

I remember two other compositions of his
on lines by the author of the "Fleurs du
Mal." One, "Le Vin de l'Assassin," is the
song of a man who has killed his wife, and
every verse ends with this exclamation by
the murderer, to which the music gives an
unspeakable and indescribable horror: "Je
l'oublierai—si je le puis."—"I will forget
her!—if I can!" In the other, entitled
"Recueillement" ("Meditation"), he had
obtained a striking effect with the lingering
and mysterious accompaniment to which he
had set that beautiful line: "Entends, ma
chère, entends la douce nuit qui marche!"
—"List, oh, my dear! list to the night's soft
step!"

I remember, too, though somewhat vaguely,
some warlike ironico-popular songs which
Villiers used to declaim with incomparable
power. He had composed them in 1870,
in collaboration with some other artists in
the same corps of *francs-tireurs*, to while
away the long night-watches of the siege;
so that the noise of the Prussian artillery,
answering our own, was their first accompani-

ment.   If I add to these short-lived works
a sort of comic opera, which never had a
definite title, but whose chief and very
ludicrous characters were a king, Paf, and
his prime minister, Toc, and the chief joke in
which was a serenade beginning with the
words :

> Si ma prière criminelle
>   Pouvait toucher les dieux retors !

> If then my criminal appeal
>   Should touch, for once, the wily gods !

I shall, I think, have pretty well exhausted
the list of the poet's compositions in the
lighter class of music.   He was no stranger
to the more serious style.   He carried in his
head (I do not believe he ever noted down
an air in his life) two complete opera scores,
choruses, orchestration, and directions for
scenery, etc., etc., etc.

One was composed on the subject of the
" Esmeralda" of Victor Hugo, so murderously
handled by Mdlle. Bertin, the other on the
" Prometheus Unbound " of Æschylus, put
into verse by my father.   Those few privi-

leged persons who, like myself, had the good
luck to hear Villiers interpret the principal
scenes of these two operas on the piano,
will, I am sure, willingly join me in declaring
that he affected them in a most unexpected
manner, and revealed, rising above numerous
gross faults and signs of musical inexperience,
many a flash of genius and beauties of the
highest order. Anybody susceptible of the
slightest artistic emotion could hardly help
being stirred, when, after a brilliant introduction, in which the tinkling of glasses, the
clash of swords, the whirl of the dance, and
the shouts of the revellers were all cunningly
mingled in seeming disorder, Villiers, in a
strident beggar's voice, began the wild opening chorus of his " Esmeralda."

Vive Clopin, Roi de Thune !
Vivent les gueux de Paris !
Faisons nos coups à la brune
Heure où tous les chats sont gris.
Dansons ! Narguons Pape et bulle ;
Et raillons nous dans nos peaux ;
Qu'Avril mouille ou que Juin brule
La plume de nos chapeaux !

Now a merry health we bring
To Paris beggars and their king !
Now we'll practise all our wiles !
On our sport old Bacchus smiles !
Merry fingers dancing snap
At Pope or bull, nor care a rap !

Let April soak or June embrown
The shabby plumes we've worn so long,
We'll gaze on them without a frown,
And turn our sorrows to a song !

Laughing at your sorry plight,
Shabby plumes we've worn so long !
Soaked by April's showers light,
Burnt by June's relentless sun !

Claude Frollo's air, with an accompaniment
of Satanic laughter, made one shiver with
horror :

Eh bien, oui ! qu'importe !
Le destin m'emporte,
La main est trop forte,
Je cède à sa loi !

*   *   *   *

Démon qui m'enivres
Qu'évoquent mes livres,
Si tu me la livres
Je me livre à toi !

O

Reçois sous ton aile
Le prêtre infidèle !
L'enfer avec elle
C'est mon ciel à moi !

For good then, or ill,
'Tis Destiny's will !
In terrified awe
I bow to its law !

*   *   *   *

Friend raised in my heart
By magic's black art !
If thou grant her to me,
I'll yield me to thee !

Receive 'neath thy wing
This priest full of sin !
All the heaven I desire
Is her kiss, in hell fire !

Having accentuated this last phrase with furious energy, Villiers would spring from his seat, in an indescribable state of excitement, and walk up and down the room, his hands raised to heaven, and his eyes flashing, repeating in every sort of tone :

L'enfer avec elle
C'est mon ciel à moi !

Very different were the sensations of the audience when the poet, lightly touching the notes with his delicate hands, began the slow, melancholy rhythm of the admirable chorus of the Oceanides in the " Prometheus Unbound," with its arpeggio accompaniment like the beating of distant wings.

(Having calmed the paternal fears)

Je t'aime, apaise ton effroi,
Sur les vents aux rapides ailes
J'arrive de loin jusqu'à toi.

A peine ai-je entendu dans notre grotte obscure
Le marteau sur le fer, que mon cœur s'est troublé.
    J'ai monté sur ce char ailé
Dans mon empressement oubliant ma chaussure,
    Et la pudeur au sein voilé.

*   *   *   *   *

Oh, corps desséché sur la pierre !
Oh, meurtrissures et douleurs !
Un nuage effrayant de pleurs
S'appesantit sur ma paupière !

I love thee ! Prithee calm thy fear !
The fleet-winged winds have brought me here,
Hastening thy trembling heart to cheer !

Scarce did I hear the hammer fall,
With iron clang, in our dark grot,
Than terror-struck, forgetting all
In my wild haste, and recking not
Of modesty, with close-veiled breast—
With feet unsandalled, bosom bare,
I sprang, obeying love's behest,
Upon my car, and clove the air.

*   *   *   *   *

Oh, wasted body on the stones !
Oh, cruel bruises, bitterest pain !
My sorrow-laden spirit groans,
And from my eyes the teardrops rain !

I have said enough, I think, about the
compositions of Villiers de l'Isle Adam to
make musicians regret that his friend Cha-
brier would never take seriously the poet's
desire that he should endeavour to note down
some of his beautiful inspirations in writing.
But in all times musicians have been jealous
of their art, and are loath to admit that an out-
sider, ignorant of fugue and counterpoint, can
do any work worth listening to. As a general
rule they may be right. But Villiers was an
exception to all rules, and it is a pity that the

composer of " Gwendoline " did not recognize
that fact.

The passion for melody used to come upon
Villiers in regular crises, attacks of music
madness which lasted from a fortnight to
three weeks.   During these periods he only
lived for counterpoint.   The only great men,
for him, were Bach, Beethoven, Mozart, and
Wagner.   Everything he wrote referred to
music.   Everything he did had music for its
end and aim.   Every piano he came across in
his nightly wanderings served him to express
his devotion to the art.   He only associated
with musicians—and such musicians! Oh, ye
gods!   My evenings at home were turned
into real splendid concerts, at which he was
at one and the same time conductor, orchestra,
accompanist, soloist, and critic!   As a pianist
he was far from attaining perfection—his
fingering and time were both bad.   As a
singer, his voice was unsteady, and often
broke ; but there was such fervour and fiery
enthusiasm and conviction in his delivery
and declamation, that in spite of his imperfections it was a deep delight to listen to him.

It was during one of these fits of music madness that he brought me a very odd couple of musicians, brother and sister—Corsicans, called, I think, Olivetti. The man was a sort of a thin sunburnt giant, with a black stubbly beard, long neglected hair falling over his shoulders, and the eyes of an incendiary. My Breton servant always locked up the plate-box as soon as he arrived. He was invariably dressed in velvet, brown, ribbed velvet, very threadbare; a huge red silk scarf was rolled round and round his neck, and he wore a soft grey felt hat, with an immense brim, victoriously cocked on one side of his head. Although a charming pianist, he was almost starving. He was a member of the "Internationale," and had been in trouble with the Italian, Russian, and French police. He had also been compromised during the Commune, and was forced to hide and to live from hand to mouth on a few ill-paid lessons and the poor salary of an accompanist to the singers in tenth-rate tea-gardens. His sister, Giulia, was a handsome soft-eyed Italian; she had a pretty soprano voice and some musical knowledge. Villiers made her sing Wagner, which she hated, and it was irresistibly funny to see and hear his bounds of rage, and angry shouts of indignation, when she would persist in warbling her Italian airs. Fortune has smiled on the pretty Giulia. A few months after I made her acquaintance she captivated and married a Chicago gentleman who had made a considerable pile of dollars by cutting up, salting, and selling pigs. She now lives in America. She took her brother there with her, and I have no doubt that he is not quite such an energetic Socialist now he has money in his pocket.

Fortunately Villiers' musical acquaintances did not all possess such a startlingly. Bohemian flavour. He owed to music a friendship and an admiration which brightened the whole of his intellectual life. His intimacy with Richard Wagner was not only a source of consolation and intellectual enjoyment to him, it inspired some of his noblest thoughts and some of the finest pages he ever wrote. The example of that marvellous and mighty genius, insulted, opposed, and scorned to his

latest hour, without this flood of hatred and
injustice ever being able to break down his
faith in his own prodigious powers, helped
Villiers to endure, on his part, the disdainful
smiles and indifference of his contemporaries,
strengthened him in his lofty disdain of those
well-beaten paths wherein mediocre intelli-
gences gather their quickly-fading laurels, and
fixed him immovably in his convictions and
his artistic faith. Though in my relation of
some facts concerning this friendship I speak
with veneration of Richard Wagner, I can no
longer hope to receive any blows in the good
cause. The author of "Tristan and Isolt"
is hallowed by fashion, and politicians no
longer dare to bring the ridiculous accusation of
lack of patriotism against his admirers. But
twenty years ago, and less, it was considered
the correct thing to run down Wagner's music
whether you were acquainted with it or not.
Nowadays no woman of fashion thinks herself complete if she does not fall into ecstasies
over the right places in "Lohengrin" and
"Tannhäuser." Every self-respecting pianist
thumps the master's overtures, and all our

young girls study Elsa, and try to ape her drooping and mystic postures. The outcast of yesterday is the idol of to-day! Well, God be praised! It is but the way of the world.

CHAPTER XIII.

First introduction of Wagner and Villiers at the house of
Charles Baudelaire—Failure of "Tannhäuser" at
the Paris Opera in 1861—Portrait and character of
Richard Wagner—His friends and champions—His
intimacy with Villiers—Reminiscences of his youth
and early poverty—Augusta Holmes—Villiers' visit
to Triebchen—The "Rheingold" at Munich—Villiers
de l'Isle Adam's artistic confession of faith.

IT was, as I think I have already said,
at the house of Baudelaire in 1861,
that Villiers de l'Isle Adam first
met Richard Wagner. This meet-
ing marks the date of what was, perhaps, the
bitterest moment in the stormy life of the
great composer. He secretly nursed a ran-
corous memory of these sufferings, and, after
the war, his unworthy and undignified abuse
of Paris betrayed the feeling. By dint of

hard work and patience, combined with his
genius, he had forced Germany to receive
and recognize him as a master in his generation.   But he was determined to have the
approval of Paris also, and offered " Tannhäuser " to the Imperial Academy of Music.
The history of his failure, complete, crushing,
almost unique in theatrical history, is known
to all.   Wagner's was one of those strange
individualities to which nobody could be indifferent; he must rouse either blind admiration or violent hatred, and he roused, alas!
more hatred than devotion.   The chorus of
evil-speaking, abuse, and scorn, which rose
from every side after the performance of his
work in Paris, would have broken down any
other man; but, unlike most others, the great
German master was never so much in his
element as in a desperate fight.   It seemed to
endow him with fresh strength and redoubled
scorn, and he generally replied to each torrent
of abuse by some proud defiance thrown in
the teeth of the tastes, the conventionality,
the prejudices, and the jealousies of the day.
At this moment, then, when Wagner was

shining with all the light of his indomitable
determination, Villiers, young and enthusiastic
as he was, met him for the first time.   This
interview never faded from his recollection.
Richard Wagner, with his high, remarkable
forehead, almost terrifying in its development,
his deep blue eyes, with their slow, steady,
magnetic glance, his thin, strongly-marked
features, changing from one shade of pallor
to another, his imperious-looking hooked nose,
his delicate,· thin-lipped, unsatisfied, ironical
mouth, his exceedingly strong projecting and
pointed chin, seemed to the poet like the
archangel of celestial combat.   And on his
side, in those hours of bitterness, the soul of
the great musician must have been strongly
drawn towards those few select spirits, who,
in spite of adverse clamour, boldly took up
his quarrel and defended and admired him.
His strong friendship with Catulle Mendès,
Baudelaire, Villiers, and a few others, dated
from this epoch ; but similarity of tastes, and a
way of looking at dreams and reality, men
and things, identical with the other's, specially
attracted the young poet and the already

grey-haired musician towards each other. They were, besides, united by a common passion for midnight walks. Wandering about, careless of weather, hour, or locality, through the mysterious sleeping streets of Paris, the two friends seldom separated before the dawn. Once, as they went down a long dreary street which ends at the Quai Saint Eustache, Wagner suddenly pointed, with a tragic gesture, to the window of a garret at the very top of a high house. There it was that he had really despaired; there he had almost died of hunger, had meditated suicide, and there, too, in the midst of the blackest poverty, he had written one of his most powerful and poetic works. He told Villiers, in that French stuffed with Teutonisms which made his conversation so odd-sounding, all the extraordinary adventures of his youth in Paris: how, towards 1839, impelled by destiny, he suddenly left Riga, in the theatre of which town he conducted the orchestra, and embarked on a sailing-ship which was going to London, intending to go thence to Paris. A fearful storm wrecked the vessel on the Norwegian coast; but Wagner did not lose courage, and reached the end of his journey. Almost unknown as he was, and in a most precarious pecuniary position, he saw the doors of the Parisian theatres scornfully shut in his face. Spurred by necessity, he tried to write ballads for the concerts, but, alas! he was not the man to write French romances, and his efforts only aroused derision. To be brief, hidden in that garret, like a fox buried in his lair, penniless, starving, he was meditating suicide, when a musical publisher came and proposed to him to arrange some operatic airs for the *cornet à piston;* and so the *cornet à piston* was the instrument of Richard Wagner's salvation! Living with the utmost economy, he contrived, by the end of a year of unexampled privation, to get together the necessary sum for hiring a piano. "I trembled in every limb," he said to Villiers, "when I first ran my fingers over the keys, but I soon found, to my exquisite joy, that I was still a musician."

And now the muse of inspiration poured out upon him the fulness of her riches. The memory of the shipwreck in which he had so lately shared, of the sea as he had seen it under the awful flashes of the tempest, the deep fiords, the bluff promontories, haunted his imagination ; then suddenly he saw, flying across the foggy Scandinavian sea swift as an arrow, illuminated by a dazzling lightning flash, the dreary ship of that legendary hero, " The Flying Dutchman." And in the bare, cold, Parisian garret, Richard Wagner, indifferent now to all physical suffering, alone with his genius, and with his shabby, hired piano, com- posed and wrote that splendid lyric poem which he christened " Der Fliegende Holländer."

But if I was to give way to the temptation of recalling all Villiers' conversations concern- ing his great and musically-gifted friend, another volume would have to be grafted on to this one of my recollections of himself. Never, indeed, was the author of " Axël " more eloquent, and indeed prolix, than when his theme was Richard Wagner. One felt that a part of the soul of the master had literally entered his ; and when he para- phrased in words some one of his works, he gave you, so to speak, an illusion of music.

In the fine book which Catulle Mendès has dedicated to the glory of the German maestro, he relates that Villiers had written down one of these paraphrases, I think the one of the prelude to " Lohengrin." I do not think it has ever been published—I have never been able to come upon it. If the former director of the " Revue Fantaisiste " has the work of his late comrade in his possession, and can be induced to publish it, he will deserve the gratitude of all lovers of literature.

Such was Villiers' passionate cultus for Wagner, that, in spite of all his poverty, I might say penury, he would contrive to make long journeys into Switzerland and Germany in order to enjoy the company, the conversation, and the music of the author of "Tristan and Isolt." During one of these distant expeditions to Triebchen, near Lucerne, he came upon a young girl whom he had already met in Paris, and whose splendid talents, now well known and uncontested, he had been among the first to recognize and applaud—I refer to Mdlle. Augusta Holmes. Villiers was enraptured at once with this young and beautiful artist, admirably gifted, filled with sacred fire, ready to make any sacrifice on the altar of art, and making light, in her sturdy confidence, of the thousand obstacles which bar a woman's entrance into the road to glory.   Long after-wards, in 1885, the great writer, in a charm-ing article, written in an enthusiastic and stirring strain, detailed his recollections of his intercourse with the young musician.   I quote two passages from it.   I must premise that Villiers saw her for the first time at Versailles, in the house of her father, Mr. Dalkeith Holmes, in the Rue de l'Orangerie, whither he had been carried off rather against the grain, by M. Camille Saint Saens, who was his companion that day :

"That evening, we heard some oriental melodies, the earliest musical thoughts of the future authoress of 'Les Argonautes,' 'Lutèce,' ' Irelande,' and 'Pologne,' and which seemed to me to be already almost free from the conventionalities of the old style of music.

"Augusta Holmes had one of those in-telligent voices which can adapt itself to any register and indicate the most delicate shades

of a musical work. I am generally inclined
to mistrust those cleverly-managed organs,
which often (to the appreciation of an un-
initiated audience) immensely heighten the
value of a commonplace composition. But
in this case the air was worthy of the accent,
and I was enchanted with the 'Sirène,' the
'Chanson du Chamelier,' and the 'Pays
des Rêves,' not to mention the 'Hymne
Irlandais,' which the young composer inter-
preted so that pine-encircled glades and
distant heaths rose before our mind's eye. It
was altogether a bright spot, musically speaking, pointing to an inevitably brilliant future.
The evening ended with some passages from
Wagner's 'Lohengrin,' lately published in
France, and to which Saint Saens introduced
us. The young composer was passionately
smitten with the new music, and her admiration for the author of 'Tristan and Isolt' has
never since belied itself."

Here is the account of the meeting at
Triebchen: "Two months before the German war I met Mdlle. Holmes at Triebchen,
near Lucerne, in Richard Wagner's own

house; her father having, in spite of his great age, decided to take the journey to Munich, in order that the young composer might hear the first part of the 'Nibelungenlied.'

"'A little less sentiment for my wishes, mademoiselle!' said Wagner, after he had listened to her with the clear-sighted and prophetic attention of genius. 'I do not want to be, to a creative genius like yours, the manchineel-tree whose shadow stifles all the birds that come within it. A word of advice! Do not belong to any school—*especially not to mine!*'

"Richard Wagner did not wish the 'Rheingold' to be played at Munich. Although the score had been published, he objected to the work being seen apart from the three other portions of the 'Nibelungenlied.' His great dream, ultimately realized at Bayreuth, was to give a representation lasting four successive evenings, of this, the great work of his life. But the impatience of his young and fanatical admirer, the King of Bavaria, had broken all bounds, and the 'Rheingold' was to be played by 'royal command.' Wag-

ner, who had refused all participation and all
assistance, anxious and saddened by the way
in which the unity of his great masterpiece
was about to be destroyed, had forbidden
any friend of his to attend the performance.
And many musicians and men of letters,
amongst them myself, who had twice travelled
to Germany to hear the master's music,
hardly knew whether to obey his distressing
injunction or not.

"'I shall look upon anybody who coun-
tenances that massacre, as my personal
enemy,' he said to us.

"Mdlle. Holmes, although driven into sub-
mission by the threat, was reduced to despair!

"However, the letter of Kapellmeister
Hans Richter, who was conducting the
orchestra at Munich, having somewhat reassured Wagner, his resentment against the
passionate zealots of his music softened, and
we took advantage of the momentary calm
to depart, almost on the sly.

"I have before me as I write a letter, and
rather a bitter one, which Wagner wrote
me to Munich, and in which he says, 'So

you have gone with your friends to see how people can *toy* with a serious work—well! well! I count on some inexterminable passages in it, to atone for much that might appear incomprehensible!'

" The predictions of the master were falsified by the brilliant triumph of the 'Rheingold'—a triumph more foreseen than actually apparent, for this opera is only fully intelligible when seen in conjunction with the three other portions of the 'Nibelungenlied,' of which it is the key.   All his adherents were present at the performance, in spite of his threats and prohibitions, and I remember seeing that night, in the first row of the visitors' gallery, Mdlle. Holmes, sitting next to the Abbé Liszt, and following the rendering of the opera in the orchestral scorebook belonging to the illustrious musician" ("Vie Moderne," Paris, 1885).

Need I add that Villiers was one of the first Frenchmen to hurry to Bayreuth in 1876, when, thanks to the sumptuous munificence of the King of Bavaria, Richard Wagner was able at last to realize his great dream.

I should like to close this veracious chronicle of the fraternal relations which existed between the great German master and the great French thinker, by quoting a page or two written by Villiers de l'Isle Adam, which, though almost unknown to scholars, would nevertheless be worthy in every way to become the fitting preface of his collected works. Villiers, in a purely imaginary conversation, put into the mouth of the beloved master, has summed up all his own artistic and religious convictions.

When we consider how hard and miserable was the life of him who poured out his soul and his conscience in this magnificent confession of an artist's faith, we can hardly read it without deep emotion.

" One twilight evening we were sitting in the darkening room looking over the garden, the rare words we interchanged, with long spaces of silence between them, scarcely disturbing our pleasing meditations, when I asked Wagner, without useless perambulation, whether it was, so to speak, *artificially* (by dint of science and intellectual power),

that he had succeeded in investing his works,
'Rienzi,' 'Tannhäuser,' 'Lohengrin,' 'The
Flying Dutchman,' even the 'Meistersinger'
and 'Parsifal,' over which he was already
brooding, with that strongly mystic quality
which emanates from them all ? Whether,
in short, he had been sufficiently freethinking
and independent of conscience to be no more
of a Christian than the subject of these lyric
dramas demanded of him ; and, finally, whether
he looked at Christianity in the same light
as that in which he viewed those Scandinavian myths, the symbolism of which he
had so magnificently illustrated in the Nibe-
lungen Ring.   This question was almost
authorized, indeed, by something which had
struck me very much in one of his principal
operas, 'Tristan and Isolt,' viz., that in
that work, in which the most intense passionate love is scornfully ascribed to the
influence of a love philtre, *the name of God
is never mentioned a single time.*

"I shall always remember the look Wagner fixed on me out of the depths of his
wonderful eyes. 'Why,' he said with a smile,

'if I did not feel in my inmost soul the living light and love of that Christian faith of which you speak, my works, which all bear witness to it, and in which I have incorporated all my mental powers, as well as the whole of my lifetime, would be the works of a liar, of an ape! How could I be childish enough to work myself up into a frenzy about what at bottom I should know to be an imposture? My art is my prayer; and, believe me, no true artist can sing otherwise than as he believes, speak but of what he loves, write otherwise than as he thinks. Those who lie, betray it in their work, which thenceforth becomes sterile and valueless, for no true work of art can be accomplished without disinterestedness and sincerity.

" ' Yes! he who for the sake of some low interests, for success, or for money, tries to make a fictitious faith stir in a so-called work of art, betrays himself, and only brings forth a corpse. Should such a traitor pronounce the name of God, not only does that name not signify to the listener what he who pronounces it would have it mean, but being, as it is, a word, and therefore a living thing, it gives, by his supreme profanation, the lie to him who utters it.   No human being can be deceived by such a device, and the author of it can only be valued at his proper worth by those of his own genus, who recognize in his want of truth that which they are themselves.

"'The first sign that marks the real artist is a burning, precise, sacred, unalterable faith ; for in every artistic production worthy of a human being, the artistic value and the living value are blended together, in the dual unity of the body and the soul.   The work of a man without faith can never be the work of an *artist*, because it will always lack that living flame which raises, enraptures, fills, warms, and fortifies the soul.   It will always be like a corpse, galvanized into life by some trivial machine.   At the same time let this be clearly understood: if, on the one hand, Knowledge *alone* can only produce clever amateurs, great inventors of "methods," of modes of action, of expressions, more or less consummately skilful in the manufacture of their mosaics, and also shameless plagiarists, who, to put one off the scent, will assimilate millions of incongruous sparks of intelligence, which lose their brightness when they re-appear out of the tinselled emptiness of such minds,—on the other hand, Faith alone can only produce and give vent to those sublime cries of the soul which, *because they cannot properly formulate themselves*, appear, alas! to the vulgar, to be but incoherent clamour. *The true artist*, he who can create, and put together, and transfigure his ideas, needs these two great gifts indissolubly united, Knowledge and Faith. As for myself, since you ask me, *above all things I am a Christian*, and the accents which touch you in my work owe their inspiration to that alone.'"

CHAPTER XIV.

EANWHILE, lost in a poor and
remote quarter of Paris, leading
a lonely existence made up of privation and sacrifices, a frail old lady
lived on, supported and consoled by her great
love for her Matthias. Yes, the old marquis
and marquise were still in the land of the

living. Poverty, age, and suffering, cold and
hunger, had not succeeded in putting out
their feeble lamp. The marquise, as I have
said, only lived for and in her son, and she
bravely endured the cruellest trials, finding her
buckler against all ills and her consolation in
all her sorrows in the worship and tenderness
of her boy. Villiers was more than a good
son—he was an admirable son. I think he
poured out all the treasures of tenderness
which were garnered in that great heart of his
upon his mother. When he spoke of his
parents, especially of her (he never did
mention them except to his closest intimates,
and those gentlemen of the boulevards never
heard him profane the sacred name of father
or of mother in their company), the tears
would come into his eyes. The moment his
pen brought him in any money, he would tear
off to the Avenue Malakoff (where the old
people inhabited two modest rooms), to share
his earnings with them, and would return
from such expeditions with a radiant face.
Nevertheless, the marquis used to cause him
some considerable trouble. Time, far from

calming the old nobleman's mania for speculation, had only intensified it.   Age and infir-
mity had not diminished his activity, and he
walked the streets from morning till night on
the look-out for wonderful opportunities.   Nobody, luckily, paid him much attention, but he
would try to insist on whirling Matthias away
with him, and making him share in the execu-
tion of the extraordinary plans he used to pro-
pound daily.   Hence arose occasional and
lively discussions, which ended in a hearty
laugh on Villiers' part, and the indignant
retirement of his father, who would exclaim,
" Well, in spite of all your talent, Matthias, you
will never be anything but an empty dream ! "
The old marquis kept his dreams and visions
as long as he lived.   The very year of his
death he wrote his son the following letter,
which depicts the extraordinary state of this
astonishing visionary's mind better than the
longest psychological study :

                    " 24th July, 1883.

" My dear Matthias,
          " We desire to make known our good

fortune to you. I hereby introduce to you, Mr. L——, who is at this moment the possessor of 25,000 francs, and who, at this time of writing, owns a well-furnished dining-room, and who is about to furnish his reception rooms with splendid pink satin curtains (which I have had in my hands), also a good piano, a superior sofa, and furniture to match. Besides this, he will have a beautiful country place, with a magnificent feudal residence with turrets, a park, fields, meadows, and vineyards, and several leagues of forest, wherein we shall be able to exercise our prowess as sportsmen. And *we* shall own (in a perfectly regular manner) some mines, the riches of which I expect you to help me to work, with our own capital.

"Your father,

"JOSEPH DE VILLIERS DE L'ISLE ADAM."

This period of Villiers' life, although the necessary investigations for the writing of "L'Eve Future" absorbed him very much, was exceedingly productive, and his literary notoriety enabled him to place his copy very easily.

He contributed tales to several daily papers which piqued themselves on their literary columns. The "Figaro," which, to its honour be it said, always liked and appreciated him, used to receive his work with deference. But his most active collaboration was given to a new magazine, "La République des Lettres," a publication too purely artistic to have any chance of longevity in this matter-of-fact century. In the office of the "République des Lettres" he found many of the friends of his earlier days, who had rallied round the former director of the "Revue Fantaisiste," Catulle Mendès. Like himself these artists were all growing old and grey in the heavy harness of life and thought. All of them had lost the greater part of their illusions, but all had preserved intact their sacred and courageous love of the ideal and the beautiful, and their indignant horror of empty platitudes. To this well-trained phalanx some youthful spirits had joined themselves, and here De l'Isle Adam laid the foundation of his friendship with a young writer of special and original talent, J. K. Huysmans. This acquaintance was to ripen, some years later, into a deep, tender, manly affection. Providence had marked out the now justly celebrated author of "A Rebours," and so many other deep and clever works, to soften by his presence and his delicate strong-heartedness the cruel death-agony of the poet. I shall return later to the subject of this intimacy.

Villiers also busied himself with collecting his scattered tales into a volume called "Contes Cruels," which, published the following year by Calmann Lévy, set the seal upon his reputation as a great artist. This work, better perhaps than any other, shows the author's complex, original, and many-sided talent. His symbolism is magnificently exemplified in such pieces of writing as "Impatience de la Foule" and "Vox Populi;" his mysticism shines brilliantly in "Vera;" his deep and bitter sense of philosophical raillery produces those strangely attractive, almost prophetic tales, "La Machine à Gloire," "L'Affichage Céleste," "L'Etna chez soi," to which last the recent anarchical struggles in Paris give a striking reality. And in those brilliant pages

of " L'Annonciateur," which even one fresh
from the perusal of Gustave Flaubert's " He-
rodias" must needs read with profound emotion, the poet and the idealist pours forth all
the overflowing wealth of his imagination.
It was concerning " L'Annonciateur " that its
author wrote : " If I think great thoughts,
people will say that what I write is fine literature ; yet it is but the clear expression of my
thought, and not literature at all ; for that has
no real existence, beyond being the clear expression of what I think."

He has elsewhere described his own idio-
syncrasy, and his destiny as an artist and a
thinker, in these remarkable and sadly symbolic terms : " Alas ! we are like some mighty
crystal vase of Eastern story, filled with the
pure essence of dead roses, and hermetically
enveloped in a triple covering of wax, of gold,
and of parchment.   One single drop of the
essence thus preserved within the precious
urn (the fortune of a whole race, handed
down by inheritance as a sacred charge,
hallowed by the ancestral blessings), suffices
to perfume many vessels of pure water, which

in their turn will embalm the air of the tomb
or dwelling wherein they are set, for many a
year.   But (and herein lies our crime) we do
not resemble those other jars filled with com-
moner perfume, scentless and melancholy phials
not worth reclosing, whose virtue weakens and
melts away under every passing breath."   It
would be wrong to imagine Villiers as a sple-
netic and silent person in everyday life, not-
withstanding the bitterness of his irony and
his immense range of thought.   He was gifted,
on the contrary, with a robust cheerfulness,
never more apparent than when he was
struggling with difficulty.   In the early days
of his Paris life, he had given rein, in all
companies, to that enjoyment of the fact of
living which expressed itself in his case by an
overflow of wit and humour.   But he soon
perceived, alas ! that the raptures of his audience were not disinterested.   When these
literary good fellows saw De l'Isle Adam
coming, they would get out their note-
books, and his sayings, his ideas for stories,
his humorous fancies, were all carefully
collected by these skimmers of the literary

pot.   So that the poor poet, opening a newspaper or magazine at random, would find his
own ideas and creations shamefully travestied
and mutilated, and impudently signed with
names which bore no resemblance to his
own.

These underhand thefts, and many another
mean treachery, poisoned a naturally sincere
and simple nature.   M. G. Guiches has very
happily reproduced the change which took
place in the poet's heart, actually affecting
even his physical appearance, in a remarkable study of Villiers de l'Isle Adam, published
in the " Nouvelle Revue," May, 1890.

" When he at last became aware of this
pilfering," says M. Guiches, " when he understood the interested object of the raptures
which used to encourage his ready tongue,
there was a sudden reaction within him.   His
soul, naturally as open as the day, shrank
within itself, his ingenuousness intrenched
itself behind a distrust as excessive as his
simplicity had once been.   His speech grew
hesitating, shorn of its former frank uncon-
strainedness. Sudden flashes of suspicion filled

his eyes with sudden shyness.   His hand was
no longer outstretched ; it waited yours, and
was only offered with the indolence bred of
disenchantment."

But when Villiers was far from the boulevard, far from professional literary men,—
when he was warmed and revived in an atmosphere of sincere friendship and admiration,—
he became himself again, and his dazzling
gaiety poured itself forth in all sorts of unexpected conceits.   It was like a perpetual
show of fireworks, and the supply of squibs
and crackers, Bengal lights and Roman
candles, used to seem inexhaustible.

He was not only a good story-teller, he
could mimic like a great and original actor,
and he thus gave the innumerable personages
created by his imagination an air of genuine,
if often fantastic reality, simulating, as he
would, their looks and voices, their gestures
and their attitudes.   Amongst all these creations, which seem as if they belong to the
dreams of Hoffman, Edgar Poe, or Dean
Swift, Villiers' favourite was always the illustrious Triboulat Bonhomet, " the son of little

Dr. Amour Bonhomet, who had adventures down in the coal mines."

During many a delightful evening, and in the course of those long midnight rambles through Paris which used to pass so quickly away in his company, I have witnessed many of the metamorphoses of that remarkable and scientific individual.   For Bonhomet, according to his creator's notion, was, while always continuing the archetype of his century, to be reincarnated in every position a man could occupy.   He was to be, turn about, professor, minister of state, police agent, philosopher, explorer, and lecturer.   I remember some of these transmigrations, which were never published, Villiers having been prevented by death from putting them into circulation.

First of all, there is a General Bonhomet, commanding-in-chief, who harangues his troops before the battle.   He points out to them that the idea of glory and patriotism is quite out of date, and calls upon them to court death in defence of agriculture, manufactures, and commerce, the three sources of the prosperity of France.   " Soldiers! let us have no more empty enthusiasm for hollow and exploded Utopias! Fight, conquer, and die for the safety of our railway system!"

Then, as a pendant to Bonhomet the slayer of swans, there was Bonhomet the erminehunter, who, having read that one of these immaculate creatures dies as soon as a stain marks its snowy whiteness, hides himself with a wonderful silent gun, charged with ink, and thus exterminates several dozen!

But the boldest conception of all is, perhaps, Bonhomet the religious man.

After a visit to Patmos, the details of which beggar all description, the doctor determines to fulfil the letter of the Scriptures, "that there shall not remain of Jerusalem one stone upon another." And having observed, as he passed through the holy places, that arches, walls, and houses were still standing, he returns to Jerusalem, accompanied by a contractor and an army of workmen, to accomplish the scriptural prophecy to the letter, and leave no stone upon its neighbour! I must not bid a final farewell to the doctor without detailing an authentic but little known anecdote, in which he plays the chief part. During the autumn of 1879, Villiers de l'Isle Adam, together with Judith Gautier, Catulle Mendès, and many other musical adepts, had gone to Bayreuth to see the divine Wagner, and assist at the performance of " Parsifal" and the " Nibelungenlied." The great master, who was all powerful at the Bavarian Court, presented Villiers to the king and his august guests, among whom was that Grand Duke who is now Czar of all the Russias. Wagner had talked so often about Triboulat Bonhomet that, willy nilly, the poet had to agree to give a reading from his works. For this purpose the whole court was assembled.

From the outset there was a murmur of stifled laughter and a rustle of unfurling fans. As the reading proceeded, the gaiety of the audience increased, growing quite noisy, and unchecked by the presence of the king, who, for that matter, laughed louder than the rest. Villiers was much astonished, and a little uneasy even, at this extraordinary hilarity. He knew well enough that his Bonhomet had a very comic side, but he never expected to

raise such a gust of merriment among personages so grave and important.   At last the
tempest of laughter rose so high that the
reader ceased and cast a glance, full of vague
suspicion, round his audience.   The Grand
Duke of Saxe-Weimar, who sat beside him,
touched his shoulder, and pointed to a person
sitting just opposite them.   Villiers, with a
little sharp cry, dropped the manuscript from
his trembling fingers, and gave evident signs
of lively terror.   There, in front of him, surrounded by a bevy of beautiful women, gazing
at him with shining eyes, his enormous mouth
open in stentorian laughter, his huge hands
leading the applause, was Dr. Triboulat Bonhomet himself, in flesh and bone (principally
bone!).   It was Liszt! From the very first
line of the manuscript, which minutely described the doctor, the whole audience had
been struck with the resemblance between
the great pianist and Triboulat Bonhomet,
and as the description went on the likeness
increased—dress, gestures, habits, all bore a
striking similarity.   One person alone did not
perceive the identity, and he laughed louder

than the rest—Liszt himself.   As the situation
worked itself out, the fits of laughter became
almost convulsing, for Villiers read on with
the most imperturbable gravity.   After this
incident *quel giorno più non si leggemmo avante!*[1]

I have spoken but little, up till now, of the
political convictions of the author of the
"Contes Cruels."   The truth is, that though
he was Royalist by racial instinct and Catholic by conviction, he considered contemporary
politics, in the depth of his heart, as a low and
vulgar science, the triumph of lying, hypocrisy
and platitude, and an end unworthy of the pur-
suit of minds inspired by the divine breath.
Nevertheless, during his short career as editor
of "La Croix et l'Epée," he constituted himself the champion of the cause of the Naundorffs.   I fancy that the strange mystery
which even now surrounds the origin of his
claim, fired the poet's imagination more than
the personal qualities of the starveling pre-
tender.

He remained a Naundorffist even after he

---

[1] "That day no further leaf we did uncover."—*Inferno*,
canto v.

was no longer at the head of the newspaper, and was convinced of the incontestability of the claims of the future Charles XI. to the throne of France. Let no one hastily conclude that this was nothing but his fancy. More serious persons than Villiers, after minute research, have shared his convictions on this head. Jules Favre, who defended the pretensions of the Naundorffs before the French tribunals, was persuaded of the rightfulness of his clients' claim. Since that time much evidence has come to light, the authenticity of which it would be hard to disprove, showing that at all events Louis XVII. did not die in the Temple. The Comte d'Hérisson, in a curious book published some years ago, and called " Le Cabinet Noir," has elucidated all this strange affair very clearly, and a perusal of his work, supported as it is by documentary evidence, is calculated to inspire doubt as to the rival pretensions of the two branches of the Bourbon family in the most incredulous and sceptical minds.[1]

[1] Since the publication of the Comte d'Hérisson's book, another has appeared on this knotty point, " L'Enfant du

However that may be, Villiers was still, in 1879, an enthusiastic partisan of the Naundorffs, when an incident which took place that year completely separated them.

A few faithful followers of the monarch in expectancy had joined together to give a dinner in his honour. Villiers was sitting, silent and absorbed, on the prince's right. Among the guests was the old Comte de F——, who for forty years had devoted everything—intellect, energy, time, and fortune—to the welfare and success of him whom he looked upon as his legitimate sovereign. The august guest lost his temper (on what account I know not) with his old and faithful servant, and, before all the assembled company, he so overwhelmed him with reproaches and abuse that the poor old man burst into sobs. A stupor of indignant astonishment fell upon the little gathering; and in the midst of the general silence, Villiers rose,

Temple," by the Baron de Gaugler, published by Savine. An authoritative work, proving the right of the Naundorffs to style themselves the descendants of the Dauphin of France.

glass in hand, and turned towards the prince. "Sire!" he said, "I drink your majesty's health. Your claims are certainly beyond dispute. You have all the ingratitude of a king!"

CHAPTER XV.

Fragments of a journal kept in 1879—A woman of
fashion bewitched—Villiers and Mar' Yvonne—A
mystery—Villiers a candidate at the elections of
the Conseil Général—Opinions of the press—
Meetings—The plans of the future councillor—
My departure from Paris—Our separation—Description of Villiers in 1880 by G. Guiches.

UNTING through old papers for
any traces I might possess of the
dear dead friend whose life I am
endeavouring to relate, I have
come across several sheets of notes, written
about this time, towards the end of 1879.
This journal is full of Villiers, with whom
I was living in almost daily intercourse,
and though it may be devoid of any other
merit, it has at all events this one, that it
was drawn from the life, and that it faithfully
reproduces my original impressions. From

it, therefore, I cull the story of one of the
last incidents in the poet's Parisian life of
which I was a witness. The reader will, I
am sure, forgive my endeavouring to vary
the monotony of my tale by the quotation :

"October, 1879. Matthias has been back
from Bayreuth for some days, and gave me
only yesterday an exemplification of the extraordinary bewitching power of his conversation over every human being who hears it.
A distant relation of my own, young, charming, elegant, and deplorably frivolous, is just
now passing through Paris. She has come
to make some purchases, to buy a *trousseau*,
and I really believe her sole mission in life
is to match ribbons and silks. God alone
knows *what* is inside the head of a young
and fashionable woman coming to Paris, with
a pocketful of money, to 'do her shopping!'
It appears to me that nothing exists for her
beyond shops, milliners, dressmakers, lace
vendors, jewellers, and so forth. Yesterday,
however, Madame de X—— was good enough
to come to my house to rest a moment, and
talk about our own part of the country.

But she had shown me her list of engagements, and made her conditions beforehand.
Half an hour by the clock, neither more nor
less, she was to spend with me.   Towards
half-past two, that is, after the first quarter
of an hour, in came Matthias, with whom she
had not been previously acquainted. . . .
Well! when Mar' Yvonne, my Breton servant,
brought in the lamp at six o'clock, my
charming cousin was still sitting on the sofa,
gazing admiringly at Villiers, who, standing
in the middle of the room, was demonstrating
to her, with unutterably comic gestures, how
the King of Bavaria valsed! Who can tell
how the miracle was accomplished ? These
performances of his beggar all description ;
they must be seen to be realized. During
yesterday afternoon Villiers played the piano,
sang, and acted through the whole of the Nibe-
lungen trilogy, interspersing his performance
with queer stories, vile puns, astonishing
reflections, and bitter jests. He imitated one
after the other, and with astonishing power,
all the august, illustrious, and crackbrained
people he had met at Bayreuth, from the

king and the princesses down to the crazy-
looking musical professors from the German
universities. He gave us a magnificent
description of the way in which the impetuous
and tyrannical maestro, Wagner, ruled the
little court with his iron rod, and lorded it
over the king just as an usher in a school
will lord it over a lower boy. He was, in
short, as he can be now and then, inimitable
and irresistible. 'Yes,' my young relative
said, 'I am furious and delighted too! I
never was so much entertained in all my
life! He is more amusing than all the Paris
theatres put together.'

"When I came back I found him disputing
with Mar' Yvonne in my bedroom. He was
turning over the contents of my wardrobe,
to choose himself some white cravats. 'Ah,
these are what I want,' he said; 'serious
ties, very serious ties, most serious ties!' He
wrapped three up in an old newspaper, and
was going away without speaking to me after
a hearty silent handshake. I tried to question him. 'Hush!—a mystery!—of capital importance! you shall know all about

it by-and-by!' and he went off bursting with laughter. There was an alarming look in his eyes which made me suspect some terrible humbug. I cross-questioned Mar' Yvonne. She said: 'I am sure, sir, that Monsieur Matthias is plotting something. He has brought me two shirts to iron, and he said to me, "You understand, Mar' Yvonne, that they must be shiny—as shiny as the inside of your saucepans!" What can it all mean? Has he any matrimonial projects?'

"November, 1879. There were no matrimonial plans, and Villiers' new mad project surpasses for comicality the best conception of the immortal Labiche. He has offered himself as a candidate in the 17th Arrondissement at the elections to the Conseil Général of the Seine, which are to take place on the 10th of next January! Nor is this all! the progenitor of Bonhomet is supported by the Royalist committee in Paris, which introduces him, patronizes him, and pays all his electioneering expenses. It seems utterly improbable, and still it is absolutely true. He has bewitched the most solemn per-

R

sonages, captivated the stiffest dowagers, and
gained the enthusiastic support of the clergy
of his parish. Those shirts and cravats were
for his meetings, of which it appears he has
already held two, both brilliantly successful.

"His adversary is the redoubtable negro,
Hérédia, a red Republican for all his black
skin. All the newspapers to-day are talking
of this unexpected candidature, and laughing
at it. The 'Figaro' is, as always, sympathetic to Villiers, but it looks upon the
whole thing as somewhat of a poetic fancy.
Some old Royalist papers, however, such as
the 'Gazette de France,' support the claims
of the great writer with many laudatory
phrases. This very day I have had a long
talk with my cousin about the whole business, and I have convinced myself that, in
spite of pleasantries and banter, he does not
at heart look upon it as at all a matter of
humbug. I am certain he has a secret hope
and desire of success. How full of contra-
diction is the human breast! This admirable
poet, this artist *par excellence*, has just let
fall to me this phrase, incomprehensible as

coming from his lips: 'After all, I hold Bulwer's opinion that the really successful man should begin by literature, go on to public life, and end in office.' Fortunately this is but a dream of ambition flitting across his mighty brain, and he will soon laugh at it himself. He has, moreover, no chance of being elected, whatever his illusions may be. He told me himself that he had somewhat alarmed some worthy delegates who interviewed him, by stating that, if he was honoured by election, he should demand, from the æsthetic point of view, the demolition of several monuments, such as the Opera House, the Church of St. Sulpice, and the Panthéon. And he also desires, with the object of providing a refuge for literary men, to obtain the re-establishment of the Debtors' Prison!"

Let me add to these fragments of personal notes the following passage extracted from an article I have already mentioned, and which was dedicated by Villiers de l'Isle Adam to the glory of Mdlle. Augusta Holmes.

"I had been chosen as the candidate of the Royalist committee at the elections for the Conseil Général of Paris, on the 10th of January, 1880. If my memory serves me, my candidature was for the 17th Arrondissement, in opposition to that redoubtable revolutionist, M. de Hérédia. It may be added, by the way, that the results of these elections, within five-and-twenty votes, being nowadays perfectly well known beforehand, I had accepted the nomination solely for the sake of the honour of being beaten.

"I obtained, as I expected, the suffrages of six hundred electors; my worthy antagonist (whose touching fugitive poetry the 'Figaro' was then publishing) obtained the resulting majority of a thousand or twelve hundred votes to which he owes his triumph; and thus both men of letters were content.

"But with regard to what concerns us just now, the amusing part of the business is this: At that time the project of an Academy of Lyric Composition for the town of Paris was already much discussed, and one evening before the great day I declared at a party, before two of the most matter-of-fact and red Republican of the councillors, that if, contrary to all expectation (for after all the election has its whims), I was successful in this venture, my first care, when the proper moment arrived, would be to point out to the commission the practical competence and usefulness of the eminent composer as a possible member of the official jury of this body. Then, with that gentle and self-satisfied smile which is so eminently characteristic of such individuals, those two guileless ones called me a poet (which always entertains me), and dismissed my project to the limbo of space. So I dubbed them prosy, in order to gratify their little vanity, and I was not at all surprised to hear that it was those two members who, if report speaks truly, influenced the commission the next year in favour of the musician, and had her placed upon the jury by an enthusiastic majority.   What poets our municipal councillors are!"

I did not see the end of this wonderful adventure.   Important family events called me back into Brittany, at the end of 1879, as

I then thought for a short visit; but providence ruled otherwise, and I have never been in Paris since, except as a casual visitor.

Thenceforward, in spite of my deep affection for Villiers, and our years of close intimacy, I only held rare communication with him, with here and there a hasty meeting rarer still. Does this imply that he was faithless-hearted? No, indeed! He had, on the contrary, what is popularly called a heart of gold. But in order to demonstrate his affection to you, he needed your bodily presence. He lived so much in the far-away land of dreams, that if you did not remind him constantly and tangibly of your existence, you came little by little to hold a vague and shadowy place in his mind, like the sweet and far-off memory of some loved and long-lost friend. And this was my fate. New elements, too, and more intimate affections, entered into his life; his increasing literary reputation brought him new friendships and new admirers, and forced him into more regular and constant literary production. His last years were certainly his fullest. Then came sickness, the hospital ward, and death, without, alas! our having met again and re-knitted the strands of our old friendship. What matter! my faith is his—that if life is hard, it is at all events short—and soon we shall meet again!

Here then end my personal reminiscences. I owe my ability to add in one last chapter some details of the poet's later life to the numerous articles concerning him published immediately after his death.   Amidst these articles, filled, many of them, with inaccuracies and absurd apocryphal stories, there is one which should fix the attention of all artists. It was published by M. G. Guiches in the "Nouvelle Revue," and has already been often referred to in the pages of this book. The young and subtle author (whose psychological researches have not withered up his heart) has succeeded perfectly in fathoming the hidden depths of the nature of the author of "Axël."   He has shown in a strikingly true and touching way the slow metamorphosis of that ingenuous nature, in the midst of the hypocrisies, the cruelties, and the villainies of life, and he has given the most admirable and speaking word-portrait of the poet that I am acquainted with. I reproduce it here. When the reader has perused it, let him turn back to the picture at the beginning of this volume, and the Villiers de l'Isle Adam of 1880, resuscitated by the magic of the pen and the art of the graver's tool, will appear lifelike before him. "He would raise his head, proudly tossing back his hair with a noble gesture, and you saw his face in all its intellectual beauty. The broad forehead, lined with parallel wrinkles, proclaimed the supreme harmony of the mental powers which had expanded it, as it were, into a superb page in the book of art. The deep depressions on the temples denoted the mathematical aptitude of which he so often gave proof. The light blue eyes bore all the external characteristics which betoken the possession of exceptional powers of memory, and the prominent eye-balls, swimming in the light of his mystic visions, or dimmed with the tears which any religious emotion or deep artistic feeling would bring to them, made his glance strangely

luminous.   All the life of the countenance had
gathered towards and remained in the upper
part of the face—the lower part was so reduced
that it seemed to disappear.   The animal or
sensual characteristics of the face were rendered invisible by the fact that the swelling
contour of the cheeks concealed the angle of
the jawbones, while the chin, hidden under a
Louis XIII. beard, betrayed by its smallness
his want of decision in practical matters.   The
slight moustache, often twisted up *à la mous-
quetaire*, was out of harmony with the expression of the mouth, full of the anxiety of a
dreamer who scents danger from afar, pursued
into the excesses of his dream by the torments
of daily life, and tasting, even yet, the bitterness and painful humiliation of the solicitations
which necessity had driven him to utter.

"From that mouth issued strange laughter, sometimes ingenuous, long and hearty,—
sometimes short and jerky,—sometimes low,
yet shrill, like the laughter of some old
savant, half-mad with learning, when he
discovers the precious meaning of some
ancient inscription, or, again, like the diabolic

gaiety of those old gnomes who are described in ancient German books as inhabiting the moss-grown belfry towers of the Father-land."

CHAPTER XVI.

THE most important event in this
part of Villiers' life is obviously
the birth of his son. The entrance
into his dreary existence of this
child, upon whom he could pour out all the

tenderness of his heart, till now jealously
treasured up, gave fresh energy and buoyancy
to the great and unhappy poet, who had imagined that all earthly happiness was ended for
him.   It is worthy of remark how much
Villiers' literary fertility gained in amount and
in regularity from this time.   Doubtless his
paternal responsibilities obliged him for the
first time to face the realities of life in a
practical fashion.

I never was acquainted with the person
who now bears the brilliant, if burdensome,
name of Villiers de l'Isle Adam.   I know
that she was without any education, of the
humblest extraction, and I am aware that the
liaison gave rise to much calumny on the part
of the poet's enemies, and much sadness and
astonishment on that of his friends.   But I
know, also, that for ten years that woman was
the brave and faithful companion of the great
artist; that she softened the closing bitterness
of his life by her affection and devotion;
that she shared his poverty, nursed him in
sickness, and that in bearing him a son she
gave him the one pure happiness that he ever

knew in this world. And I know, lastly, that Villiers de l'Isle Adam, lying on his deathbed, on the very brink of eternity, did not think this humble companion unworthy of that supreme act of self-sacrifice by which he gave her the right to bear his name before God and men. For all these reasons, the widow of Villiers has a right to the deference of all admirers and friends of her late husband, and I believe I shall best show mine by wrapping the story of this *liaison*, which after all concerns nobody but the actors in it, in respectful silence.

As soon as little Victor ("Totor," as he was called in the intimacy of his family circle) had left his first baby lispings behind him, and was able to toddle a little, he became the constant companion of his father's walks. In the daytime one was seldom to be met without the other, and there used to be something at once comic and touching in Villiers' delight, astonishment, and admiration over the prattlings of his little son.

The "Contes Cruels," published by Calmann Lévy, appeared in 1881, and in spite of the in-

difference of the Parisian public to all really
artistic work, the book was too powerful and
too original not to create a certain amount of
sensation. Some of the chief critics scornfully
gave the work a few laudatory sentences, and
straightway the press followed like a flock of
sheep. So great is the power of journalism
that a few weeks made Villiers famous. He
took advantage of this revival of popularity to
place his copy in various papers and magazines,
and thus earn a little money. Meanwhile
" L'Eve Future" was nearly finished. Some
of his friends, knowing the writer's difficulties,
proposed to occupy themselves with the endeavour to get this, the crowning effort of his
literary life, published as a serial. Although
the idea of seeing his work cut up and served
to the public in daily slices made Villiers
shiver with horror, he accepted, driven by
hard necessity. It was the " Gaulois " which
had the idea of offering the profound and
startling work of the gifted writer as intellectual food to its readers—all of them habitual
admirers of Ohnet, Tarbé, and Montépin.
The issue had to be stopped at the tenth

number, for the middle-class public left off subscribing in swarms.   The disappointment was not great to Villiers, who had always looked upon the appearance of "L'Eve Future" in the serial columns of the "Gaulois" as a sort of gigantic joke.   It was not till two years later (in 1884) that his book found a setting worthy of it in the beautiful and luxuriously got-up review, "La Vie Moderne," then published by Charpentier.   Villiers eventually became one of the most assiduous contributors to this truly artistic publication.

I will only mention in the most summary manner the ridiculous performance of the "Nouveau Monde," which took place at the Théâtre des Nations in 1883.   There is no use now in raking up old quarrels; but Villiers was cruelly played upon and shamefully deceived on that occasion.   He ought never to have allowed his play to see the footlights under conditions which made its failure a foregone conclusion.   I was not present on the opening night.   There were six performances.   Mdlle. Rousseil was simply grotesque, and I have been assured that she acted badly on purpose. One of my brothers was present, one evening, at the massacre, and he told me that the hubbub in the auditorium was deafening. Villiers led the clamour, armed with a huge key, on which he whistled noisy Tyrolean airs. This remarkable historical drama, perhaps the finest ever written on that particular subject, still awaits the good pleasure of some intelligent and artistic manager. But I hardly know whether that rare bird exists in France.

A cruel and twofold separation, rendered, however, less cruel by his strong religious faith, was reserved to Villiers in the end of 1883. The two lights which had for so many years cast a ray of warm affection over his otherwise dreary life, went out, almost suddenly, one after the other. The marquise and the marquis died quietly at a few months' interval in their little dwelling in the Avenue Malakoff. Life had not been unfriendly to them on the whole. The marquis till his last hour lived in his brilliant dreams, deaf and blind to all reality, seeing each day in some fascinating mirage the fortune and the glory he was to attain—the next!

The illusions of the marquise were more silent and tenderer, all concentrated as they were on her Matthias. In her day-dreams she saw him crowned with an aureole of glory, and the plaudits of the newspapers (their dagger-thrusts were always concealed from her by his filial tenderness) beguiled till its last throb that heart so absorbed by maternal love. Poor Villiers wept sorely, prayed devoutly at the bedside of his dead parents, spent all the money he possessed (not much, poor fellow!), in having them fittingly buried, and then went back with a burst of passionate tenderness to his little " Totor."

It was at this moment that he gave up living in furnished lodgings, having inherited from the old couple their simple furniture, amongst which survived one or two remnants of former grandeur, a grand piano by Pape, and a Louis XV. table with fine copper mounts.

Providence owed Villiers some compensation for such bitter sorrows, borne with so much Christian resignation; and if the void

caused by the loss of his parents was never
entirely filled, yet some strong and con-
siderate friendships, which surrounded him
even on his deathbed, did much to lessen it.
Among these friends, none was more useful
and more congenial to him than M. J. K.
Huysmans. Until the year 1884, the two
writers had frequently met at close quarters
without making acquaintance. Each was
afraid of the other's exterior, and neither
realized their great psychological and intellectual resemblance. This resemblance
was, however, not identical. For while Villiers allowed his dreams to eddy at the mercy
of contrary winds across the broad sphere of
speculative thought, Huysmans, more master
of his own thoughts, and holding the reins
of his imagination even in its wildest flights,
condensed his into one of the strongest,
most original, best conceived and best exe-
cuted books of modern times. I allude to
" A Rebours."

Knowing as I did the innermost depths
of Villiers' nature, I can imagine, judging
from my own sensations, what exquisite

pleasure the perusal of this fascinating book must have given him. I can see his blue eyes fill with tears as he turns over those pages instinct with living and immortal art. Such emotions are amongst the noblest and most beautiful in life! But that which must have specially touched Villiers is that the accomplished writer had devoted an important passage in his book to the author of " L'Eve Future." I reproduce here, shortening it a little, Huysmans' opinion of the works of Villiers de l'Isle Adam. But I should state that it was formed before the publication of his two masterpieces, " L'Eve Future " and " Axël."

" He then turned his attention to Villiers de l'Isle Adam, in whose scattered works he still noted some seditious passages, and in which some thrills of morbid emotion still vibrated, but which, with the exception at least of 'Claire Lenoir,' no longer shed such an overwhelming sense of horror on the reader. This last story was evidently inspired by those of Edgar Poe, whose love of close discussion and taste for the horrible it

reproduces.   The same might be said of
'L'Intersigne,' which was later on inserted
in the 'Contes Cruels,' a collection of tales of
indisputable talent, amongst which was one,
'Vera,' which Des Esseintes [the hero of
Huysmans' book] looked upon as a masterpiece in miniature.   In this last the fanciful-
ness of the story is full of an exquisite
tenderness.   We no longer have the gloomy
phantoms of the American author, but a
warm, translucent, almost celestial vision, the
opposite, though in an identical style, of
Beatrice and Ligeia, those pallid spectres
raised by the inexorable nightmare of the
opium-eater.   This story also treats of the
operation of the human will, but not as
to its weaknesses and failures, under the
influence of terror.   It studies, on the contrary, its excitement under the impulse of a
conviction, developing into a fixed idea, and
demonstrates that power which succeeds even
in pervading the very atmosphere, and im-
posing its will on intangible things."

"But," he went on to say, "there exists
another side in the temperament of Villiers,

far more keen and clearly-defined—a side of gloomy jesting and cruel raillery. This gives rise, not to the paradoxical mystifications of Edgar Allan Poe, but to that sad banter of the heavy-hearted jester in which Swift revelled.

"One series of short pieces, 'Les Demoiselles de Bienfilatre,' 'L'Affichage Céleste,' 'La Machine à Gloire,' 'Le plus beau dîner du monde,' reveal a power of banter of a singularly bitter and inventive order. All the impurity of contemporary utilitarianism, all the ignominy of the century, are glorified in these works, whose pungent irony so delighted Des Esseintes."

A little further on, in an anthology which Des Esseintes has had printed for his own use—"a little chapel with Baudelaire as its patron saint"—we find the "Vox Populi" of Villiers : "A superb coin, struck in a golden mould, with the effigies of Leconte de L'Isle and of Flaubert."

This great book, "A Rebours," was the bond which united Huysmans to Villiers de l'Isle Adam in what was to prove a lasting friendship, the tender consideration and manly affection of which was most beneficial to the latter, softening to him many a blow, many a bitterness, and many a humiliation.

If he had lived long enough it might have given him a taste for a regular, sober, retired and studious existence, and have drawn him away by degrees from the terrible manner of life which ended by consuming his strength. But it was too late. By the time Huysmans knew him, death had marked him for his own!

Villiers de l'Isle Adam produced a great deal between the publication of the " Nouveau Monde" and that of " L'Eve Future" (1883 to 1886). First of all came " Triboulat Bon-homet," the first volume of a long series he projected, which was to relate with minute detail all the adventures and discoveries of the worthy doctor. This is how the author expresses himself on the subject in the preface placed at the head of this work :

"We first of all, in order to initiate the public into the character of Doctor Bonhomet, give three tales which illustrate in a general manner his individual peculiarities.

"Next, the doctor himself takes up his parable and tells us the more than strange story of 'Claire Lenoir,' the heavy responsibility for which we leave entirely on his shoulders. If, as we have some reason to fear, this personage, whose actual existence is incontestable, obtains some popularity, we shall soon publish, not without regret, certain anecdotes of which he is the hero, and certain aphorisms of which he is the author."

This volume, besides "Claire Lenoir," contains the admirable ironical allegory of Bonhomet the swan-hunter, "The Paper of Dr. Triboulat Bonhomet on the 'Utilization of Earthquakes,'" and the "Banquet of the Eventualists."

"Triboulat Bonhomet" was followed by "Propos d'au-dela" (1 vol., published by Brunhoff), and the superb prose poem, "Akëdysseril," which reproduces in realistic fashion the dazzlingly splendid visions of the East Indies. Then, almost simultaneously with "L'Eve Future," another dreamy work,

full of dignity and sadness, "L'Amour Su-
prème," appeared at the same publishers,
and, in 1886, "L'Eve Future" in its final
form appeared in the booksellers' shop-fronts
garbed in a whimsical covering. Villiers
gave the key to this book when he dedicated
it " To dreamers and to scoffers." Its pages
are indeed the lists in which those two champions, fancy and irony, struggle eternally
together without either coming out the victor.
The author wrote for this book, the most important work of his literary life, a long preface,
the first part of which only was published at
the beginning of the volume. M. G. Guiches,
in the remarkable study from which I have
already frequently quoted in the course of this
work, has reproduced the original text in its
entirety. I will only cite the following frag-
ment: "I know no precedent for my book,
none like it, nor analogous to it. Whether
it arouses anger or merely meets with indifference, I do not think it will be utterly forgotten, for in truth its gloomy pages do not
treat of the famous ' De omni re scibile,' but
rather of the ' et quibusdam aliis.'"

The appearance of " L'Eve Future" caused a sort of stupor of astonishment amongst the ranks of the critics. These gentlemen really did not know what to say to it. It was not like anything that was generally written, and, besides, Villiers' reputation made them fear some mystification. Yet it was impossible to deny that this one book contained more imagination, more scientific knowledge, and more art than all the other works appearing at the same time put together. The reviewers, to get out of their difficulty, launched into vague praises or puerile jests, diluted with sugary compliments, and all of them, without much understanding it, acclaimed the "incontestable intellectual superiority of this original conception."

Villiers was forthwith consecrated a great writer, his renown crossed the Channel, and penetrated across the frontier, causing much preoccupation in Belgium, that literature-loving country, always on the watch for whatever succeeds in France. The following year an association for providing courses of lectures on different subjects, having its headquarters at Brussels, made lucrative offers to the author of "L'Eve Future." Villiers, although he was already sorely stricken by the malady which was eventually to carry him off, gladly accepted this opportunity of publicly enunciating his ideas on men and art. He started, and had not occasion, like Baudelaire, to complain of his reception by the worthy Belgians. His success was very great. Some hasty notes, written by him to a friend, and published by M. Guiches in the "Nouvelle Revue," enable us to follow the course of his triumphs. I reproduce them here. I should add, to make matters clear, that Villiers had left Paris just at the moment that a new collection of his tales, "Les Histoires Insolites," was about to appear at Quantin's.

"My dear M——,

"I write in great haste. I cannot send to the 'Gil Blas' for the note till to-morrow, as I have just come in from a lecture, and am very tired in spite of the astonishing success I have had.

"I beg of you (in great haste, post just going) to send out the presentation copies with the publisher's compliments, in the author's absence. This is constantly done. I can yet earn 800 francs by lectures here, so I cannot come back so soon. But I will give up the whole of to-morrow to drawing up notes and other matters for the book. And I have, besides, all the proofs of another book to correct right off.

"At least 500 copies have been sold in advance in Belgium through my lectures, at which I have read, or am about to read, extracts. I go on Tuesday to Liège, then to Antwerp, Ghent, etc., and shall be in Paris in less than ten days. Greetings!"

"My dear M——,

        "You send me no books, and yet you have no idea of the enthusiasm with which I am received here, nor that two or three hundred book-lovers are buying my works, which, rightly or wrongly, do not seem to have been written solely to be used for lighting fires. The newspapers say wonderful things of me, and I am very much pleased I am giving lectures in several towns, and hope to bring back a little money. I shall not be able to start back till Saturday or Sunday. It cannot be possible that the 'Histoires Insolites' are not even stitched yet. Hearty greetings!

"VILLIERS.

"P.S.—I have already caught the Belgian accent!"

"My dear Friend,

"Great haste, post just off. Huge success, five recalls, the queen, etc. Three columns about me in every paper. I am at the Grand Hotel, No. 147.

"Hasty greetings!
"VILLIERS DE L'ISLE ADAM.

"P.S.—Send the 'Histoires Insolites' for lecture."

Thus did fortune, so long perverse towards the poet, consent at last to shower her smiles upon him. Alas! she only did it to make the final blows she was preparing to deal him seem more cruel! She hated this great gentleman, this poet, who had always borne with magnificent scorn the deepest wounds she gave him, scarce feeling them, indeed, thanks to that sovereign balm of fancy which had been given to him at birth by his god-mother, the fairy queen of the ideal. And now, to avenge herself for all his disdain, she was about to call the forces of agonizing physical suffering to her aid.

Everything smiled on Villiers in that year 1888. He was free from want; he had grown famous; publishers received him with a friendly smile; he heard himself addressed as "Master" at the evening parties at Charpentier's; the smaller fry of the literary world buzzed flatteringly around him. "Axël" (in the "Revue Indépendante") was making a great stir. His books, the "Histoires Insolites" and the "Nouveaux Contes Cruels," were being bought. He himself was astonished at the sudden reaction. And lo!—sickness came upon him like a terrible, implacable enemy, threw its arms about him, overthrew him, cast him on his bed groaning, shivering, lost and convulsed in agonizing suffering. A short time before, the poor poet, weary of Paris, and longing for green woods and water, had retired to Nogent-sur-Marne; and thither death sent his pale-faced emissaries to take possession of him.

Another pen, reader, more worthily than mine, will tell you how he left Nogent for the house of the Brothers of St. Jean de Dieu; how his last hours passed there, and how he died, after accomplishing a final sacrifice worthy of all his life. For I have appealed to one who was the deeply-moved witness and the chief support of Villiers' last agony, the last to bid him farewell on the shores of eternity, to relate in all its true and heartbreaking details the story of the poet's end.

M. Huysmans understood the motive of my request, and he has consented, in spite of its bitterness, to revive the memory of the sad hours spent by that deathbed, for the sake of paying a last homage to his friend and comrade. Here is his letter:

"Paris, *April* 21, 1892.

" Dear Sir, and Brother Writer,

"You are by no means a stranger to me. I have read your words about Villiers in ' L'Hermine,' and several times, if my memory does not deceive me, our late friend mentioned you to me. I knew, therefore, that I had to do with one whose outward appearance only was unfamiliar, when Landry[1] spoke to me of the book you thought of writing.

"Villiers was very dear to me, and like you (especially on evenings when I have had to endure some very empty chatter) I am haunted by the presence of him who certainly may be bracketed with Barbey d'Aurevilly as the two most astonishing conversationalists of our day. I first knew him many years ago (in 1876) at the house of Catulle Mendès, who managed the ' République des Lettres,' on which we were both writing. But our

---

[1] M. G. Landry, head clerk to M. Savine, the bookseller, whom I cannot sufficiently thank for the sympathy, help, and information he has given me during the writing of my book.

friendships and our tastes alike differing, we soon drifted apart. We met again after the publication of 'A Rebours,' and thenceforward, far from the boulevards, our friendly relations recommenced. He used to come on Sundays, with his child, little Totor, to dine with me, and these occasions were memorable ones to those who met him. Suspicious, and justly on the defensive as he generally was when he met literary people, the hesitating mode of expression in which he usually took refuge the moment he felt he had let himself go too far, was laid aside in the congenial atmosphere of faithful friendship and true admiration; and, safe from any fear of plagiarism or treachery, he would launch out and talk about his own life, in a fashion at once poetic and realistic, ironical and madly gay.

" I remember, in this connection, one 14th of July, when he came and dined with the father of Lucien Descaves, at Montrouge. After dinner, he sat down to the piano, and, lost in a sort of dream, he sang, in his cracked and quavering voice, bits of

Wagner, mixed up with choruses of barrack songs, and joining all together with strident laughter, wild jokes, and quaint rhymes.

"But nobody ever had such a talent for raising and transforming a joke into something far beyond its apparent scope, and even beyond the widest range of possibility. There was a punchbowl always flaming, as it were, in his brain. How often have I seen him in the morning, just out of bed and hardly awake, holding forth as brilliantly as when of an evening he would tell us astounding anecdotes and inimitable stories over our coffee!

"But our meetings grew rarer. Sickness prostrated him, laid him shivering in his bed. Weary of Paris, he settled at Nogent, and soon grew worse. Dr. Robin recognized the symptoms of cancer, but disguised the truth, asserting that the malady was one of the digestive organs, and fortunately Villiers believed him. One day that he was more suffering than usual, the sick man complained to me about the house he was in. It was, as a matter of fact, as cold as a cellar, sunless, almost rotted with damp. He said he would like to leave

T

it, and added that he needed skilful nurses to turn and move him in his bed. I mentioned the Brothers of St. Jean de Dieu in the Rue Oudinot in Paris, and two days later I had a letter from him saying he was settled in their house, thanks to the mediation of Coppée with the director, which obtained for him exceptionally easy terms of admission. I found him there delighted with the change, convinced of his speedy recovery, full of plans, amongst others to give up going to the *brasseries* on the boulevards and to work quietly in some corner far from the buzz of journalism.

" He who had been so unlucky and so poor all his life was now in comparative affluence, and no longer haunted by detestable pecuniary anxieties. Mallarmé, a very sincere and attentive friend, had opened a secret subscription for him, and I, on my part, had at my disposal a tolerable sum which the faithful Francis Poictevin had confided to me with the same object.

" Villiers began at this time to talk about ' Axël,' which was then on the stocks, and which he desired to remodel, suppressing some theories in it which, from the Catholic point of view, he thought were unorthodox. And then suddenly he grew silent. For the first time, perhaps, in his life, that gift of fancy, which had enabled him to forget all the endless sufferings of life in the fairyland of his imagination, failed him. He beheld life as it really is, understood that cruel reality was about to wreak her vengeance on him, and then his long martyrdom began.

" The digestive functions ceased to work, his strength failed, his emaciation became frightful. A sort of straw-coloured shadow crept over his features, and in the wasted face the eyes lived on, seeming to pierce the very soul of the onlookers with their terrifying glance. In spite of the efforts of Madame Méry Laurent, a friend who nursed him and petted him, bringing him the most nourishing food and authentic wines, he could not eat, and death approached with rapid strides.

" And here must come in the sad episode of his marriage. For reasons which he did not disclose, Villiers hesitated, hung back,

would not answer when we spoke to him
timidly, and with much circumlocution, about
his little son, and suggested that in order
to legitimize the child he should marry the
mother, with whom he had long lived. Impelled by our argument, that probably after
his death the Minister of Public Instruction
would grant a pension to the child that bore
his name, he at last consented. But when
it came to fixing the day and getting the
necessary papers together, he put us off,
raised objections, and finally shut himself
up in such obstinate silence that we had to
be silent too. The friends who were in the
habit of visiting him, Madame Méry Laurent,
Stéphane Mallarmé, Léon Dierx, Gustave
Guiches, and I myself, did not know what
wiles to employ to induce him to yield. He
was growing hourly weaker, and we began
to fear he would die before we could get the
documents necessary for the marriage together. Sick with anxiety, it occurred to me
one morning to apply to the almoner of the
Brothers of St. Jean de Dieu, a Franciscan
from the Holy Land, the Rev. Père Sylvestre.

He was a gentle and compassionate monk,
who had already helped Barbey d'Aurevilly
to die. I reminded him of the lamentable
story, which he already knew, for Villiers had
confessed to him and received the communion
from his hand.

"He simply answered : 'Well, just wait
for me there. I will go up and say a word to
him.' Five minutes later, he left the sick-
room, and Villiers had consented to an immediate marriage.

"Time pressed, and it was difficult to get
hold of the certificates which were scattered
about in different registry offices. Of the few
friends who still remained faithful to him (his
café and newspaper acquaintances had of
course long since abandoned him), the only
ones left in Paris were Léon Dierx, who was
shut up all day in his office, Gustave Guiches,
and myself. It was summer-time. Mallarmé
was ill, and had fled to the country. Madame
Méry Laurent was away taking waters.
There was a wild hunt after the necessary
documents. Guiches and M. de Malherbe (a
clerk at Quantin's bookshop, who was to be

one of the wife's witnesses) devoted themselves
to it, and between the three of us, with the
help of an employé at the Mairie of the
7th Arrondissement, M. Raoul Denieau, an
admirer of Villiers, who smoothed down many
difficulties which we should have stumbled
at, we contrived on the very day appointed
for the marriage to bring together the necessary certificates.   The marriage took place in
the sick-room.   And here I hesitate somewhat
to reveal the whole truth.   But you will make
whatever use you think right of this letter,
and you will judge whether, amongst the facts,
all of them absolutely true, which I send you,
to strengthen the authoritative accuracy of your
book, these particular ones should be given to
the public.   On the whole, I think myself that
they should—for the details of the suffering
of such a man as Villiers are worth learning.

" When it became necessary to sign the registers, the wife stated that she did not know
how to write.   There was a terrible moment
of silence.   Villiers lay in agony with his eyes
closed.   Ah! he was spared nothing.   His
cup overflowed with bitterness and humilia-

tion! And while we were all looking at each
other, almost broken-hearted, the wife added :
'I can make a cross as I did for my first
marriage.' And we took her hand and helped
her to make the mark. After the ceremony
the four witnesses, Mallarmé, Dierx, M. de
Malherbe, and I, tasted a little champagne
which Villiers insisted on offering to us. Then
the Rev. Père Sylvestre came to celebrate the
religious marriage. And then it was that we
had an opportunity of realizing the priest's
kindness of heart. Villiers' wife used to
spend the day with him. In spite of her
false position, the Brothers of St. Jean shut
their eyes to this infringement of the letter of
their rules. But of course her visits had to
end with the day; she had to leave at twilight,
and this was a heartbreak to the unhappy
man, who dreaded dying alone in the night.
When he had pronounced the marriage benediction, the Rev. Père Sylvestre said in rather
a hurried voice, 'Although women are not
allowed to spend the night here as a rule,
I have obtained permission that now you are
married you shall not be separated àgain.'

The monk had thought of giving this last happiness to the dying man. Villiers' eyes filled with tears; he made a gesture, then fell back exhausted, almost fainting from fatigue, and we left him.

"I went to see him the next day, and all the following days. He could no longer speak, but would squeeze your hand gently, and look at you with great sad patient eyes. The evening before his death he received the last sacrament, and lay half-conscious, his wan face grown hollow and his throat rattling. I felt the end was very near, but overwhelmed as I was I had to hurry away, for it was very late, and the convent was closing for the night.

"A ring at the bell early next morning made me jump out of bed. 'Villiers is dead,' I said to myself, and it was too true. His wife sank sobbing into a chair in my room.

"What more shall I say? Better say nothing of the literary vultures who settled on that corpse, of the reporters who used to come daily to await his decease and place their wares, who were now able to draw their pay, and cease their constant calls of inquiry.

" Little use either in telling you about the funeral, at which the mourners, Mallarmé, Dierx, and I, sheltered the poor unconscious orphan boy as best we could from the pelting rain. And yet I will say one other word concerning that funeral ceremony, at which the Rev. Père Sylvestre pronounced the benediction, in the Church of St. François Xavier. Our own resources being exhausted, we applied, Gustave Guiches and I, to the office of the 'Figaro,' and M. Magnard, with a kindly courtesy which I never can forget, offered to place at our disposal the sum necessary to defray the expenses of the decent burial of our friend.

" Others, my dear sir, will give you more complete information concerning Villiers' life, and will furnish you with the details of that extraordinary existence, starving, forlorn, penniless, and clouded by troubles so great as to make his condition at times without parallel in its misery. I have confined myself to those sad incidents which immediately preceded his death, and, as you have narrated the beginning of his life, so I relate to you its close.

" In conclusion, dear sir, I have to wish your book good luck, and I do it with all my heart.   May your work kindle some spark of regret for its own injustice in that public which so resolutely refused to acknowledge the talent of Villiers before his death.

"Believe me, etc.,

" J. K. HUYSMANS."

The next day, Tuesday, 20th August, 1889, a few hours before the burial, M. Henri de Lavedan, a young writer whom Villiers de l'Isle Adam had inspired with one of those enthusiastic attachments which he alone could create, asked permission to gaze once more on the features of the dead man who had been so dear to him, and prayed long in the quiet little room.   I desire to place here, as the conclusion of the work in which I have endeavoured to outline the life of that great believer and great artist, the Comte Philippe Auguste Matthias de Villiers de l'Isle Adam, these lines instinct with deep and sincere feeling, which were written immediately after this farewell visit :

"On an August morning, wet and dreary as a November evening, in the house of the Brothers of St. Jean de Dieu, which stands in the quiet quarter of the 'Invalides,' the brown-robed monk gently closed the door behind me, and I saw before me Villiers de l'Isle Adam lying on his deathbed. We are alone together, he and I. The little room is very quiet, clean with the cleanliness of the cloister and the death-chamber—coldly calm. On the chimney-piece the flame of the candles burns high and motionless, undisturbed by any breath of air ; and the half-closed eyes of the gifted scoffer who shall scoff no more, gazing lifelessly at the coffin waiting on the floor, seem to contemplate it as though it were a friend. I kneel on a *prie-dieu*, and gaze on the face of the master I have known and loved. The narrow bed on which he died is all too wide for his poor body, ema-ciated by long and cruel suffering. But the

proud and beautiful head, whose great forehead seems to have been carved out by death
for posterity in the firmest and whitest of
marbles, stands out with a royal dignity.
Sightless and voiceless as it is, bereft of
thought, of everything that made it glorious,
that splendid head still seems to fill the room.
It seems to be the head of him who Villiers
would have been, had he lived, and fought,
and sung, in one of those ages of faith which
he loved, and loved with the bitter love of the
exile.   It was as solemnly beautiful under the
shadow of those cotton curtains, as it would
have been under a gold-fringed daïs, and I
could have fancied I beheld the corpse of one
of his ancestors, a Villiers de l'Isle Adam of
the crusading times, who, worn out by fever,
fatigue, long marches, wounds, and thirst, had
at last, on some burning shore of Palestine,
rendered up his gallant soul to God who
called it.

" Visions and beliefs.   These were the
whole of Villiers' being.   As I looked at
him lying there with a poor rosary in his
folded hands, his whole frame stretched out

with a tired air (betokening as much weari-
ness as resignation), I could not but remember
that he was a steadfast Christian, believing,
and practising what he believed.   It was his
faith alone which kept him straight to the
end of the book of his life, to the last line,
and to his last breath, without a blot on the
escutcheon which descends to his son as stain-
less as he inherited it from his own father.

   " And I imagine that the severe and noble
expression on the calm features of this Christian man of letters comes of the joy of feeling
he is free, delivered at last from this life of
emptiness, of folly, of many pangs, which
brought him nothing, neither health, nor
wealth, nor love, nor glory.

   " Death did not come upon Villiers un-
awares; he watched its slow approach with
perfect calmness. He bore the Cross of Malta;
he was well prepared to meet the King of
Terrors, and when he drew near and stood
before him, he received the accolade fearlessly,
like a soldier and a gentleman, hoping perhaps
that his reward was beginning.   He knew, in
his humble trust, that the hour had come for

his own judgment on high, for that of his work here below, and doubtless he repeated mentally that motto of Hassan-ben-Sabbah which he placed at the head of his own poem, ' Azraël '—' O Death ! those who are about to live salute thee ! ' "

FINIS.

CHISWICK PRESS :—C. WHITTINGHAM AND CO.
TOOKS COURT, CHANCERY LANE.

Telegraphic Address:
Sunlooks, London.

21 BEDFORD STREET, W.C.

December 1893

A LIST OF

MR. WILLIAM HEINEMANN'S

PUBLICATIONS

AND

FORTHCOMING WORKS

Index of Authors.

In Two Volumes, 4to.

REMBRANDT:

HIS LIFE, HIS WORK, AND HIS TIME.

BY

ÉMILE MICHEL,

MEMBER OF THE INSTITUTE OF FRANCE.

TRANSLATED BY

FLORENCE SIMMONDS.

EDITED AND PREFACED BY

FREDERICK WEDMORE.

With 33 photogravures, 34 coloured reproductions of paintings and chalk drawings, and 250 illustrations in the text.

THE ORDINARY EDITION. Printed on superfine paper specially made for this work, price £2 2s. *net.*

THE EDITION DE LUXE. Limited to 150 numbered copies for Great Britain, printed on specially imported Japanese vellum, with India proof duplicates of the photogravures, price £10 10s. *net.*

Nothing need be said in justification of a comprehensive book upon the life and work of Rembrandt. A classic among classics, he is also a modern of moderns. His works are to-day more sought after and better paid for than ever before; he is now at the zenith of a fame which can hardly decline.

The author of this work is perhaps, of all living authorities on Rembrandt, the one who has had the largest experience, the best opportunity of knowing all that can be known of the master.

The latest inventions in photogravure and process-engraving have enabled the publisher to reproduce almost everything that is accessible in the public galleries of Europe, as well as most of the numerous private collections containing specimens of Rembrandt's work in England and on the Continent.

An illustrated prospectus may be had on application.

Autumn Publications.

MEMOIRS.
By CHARLES GODFREY LELAND
(HANS BREITMANN).

In Two Volumes, 8vo.   With Two Portraits.   Price 32s.

CONTENTS.—Early Life, 1824-1837.   Boyhood and Youth, 1837-1845.
University Life and Travel in Europe, 1845-1848.   The Return to
America, 1848-1862.   Life during the Civil War and its Sequence,
1862-1866.   Life on the Press, 1866-1869.   Europe Revisited,
1869-1870.   England, 1870.

The Times.—From first to last a very entertaining book, full of good stories,
strange adventures, curious experiences, and not inconsiderable achievements,
instinct with the strong personality of the writer, and not unpleasantly tinged
with the egotism that belongs to a strong personality."

THE ROMANCE OF AN EMPRESS.
CATHERINE II. OF RUSSIA.
By R. WALISZEWSKI.

Translated from the French.   In Two Volumes, 8vo.   With Portrait.
Price 32s.

M. Waliszewski's book is based upon unpublished documents in the State
archives, and upon the memoirs and correspondence of his subject.   There has
been no more extraordinary figure in Russian history than this gifted, tem-
pestuous, and dissolute empress, "the Semiramis of the North."   The story of
the plots and intrigues, the wars and triumphs, the succession of favourites, and
the fierce outbreaks with which her reign was filled, reads like the half-mythical
chronicle of a king of Babylon or one of the earlier Moguls.   It is a most extraordinary historical romance which M. Waliszewski has written, and it presents
some fresh aspects of European history.

A FRIEND OF THE QUEEN.
MARIE ANTOINETTE AND COUNT FERSEN.
By PAUL GAULOT.

Translated from the French by Mrs. CASHEL HOEY. In Two Volumes,
8vo. With Two Portraits, Price 24s.

The interesting and brilliant life of the French Court towards the close of
the eighteenth century, with the varied figures of historical and personal interest, are nowhere so closely depicted as in this account of the relations
existing between Marie Antoinette and the fascinating young Swedish nobleman,
Count Axel de Fersen, whose romantic friendship with the ill-fated Marie
Antoinette led him gladly to peril his life again and again in vain attempts at
rescue.   The hero of Court *fêtes* in the palmy days of Louis XVI., a soldier in
the American Revolution and an aide-de-camp at Yorktown, the disguised
coachman of Marie Antoinette in the flight which ended so wretchedly at
Varennes, the agent of Gustavus III. in the attempts to reinstate the Bourbons,
the favourite of Charles XIII., and the Grand Marshal of Sweden, and finally
the victim of mob fury killed like a mad dog with sticks and stones in Stockholm
—here, surely is a career to which history offers few counterparts.   The main
facts are known.   The details which lend colour and throw a new light on many
historical points have been obtained for this volume from family archives.

Third and Cheaper Edition.

ALFRED, LORD TENNYSON.

A STUDY OF HIS LIFE AND WORK.

By ARTHUR WAUGH, B.A. Oxon.

With Twenty Illustrations from Photographs specially taken for this
Work, Five Portraits, and Facsimile of Tennyson's MS.
Crown 8vo. Cloth gilt edges, or uncut, 6s.

CONTENTS. — Lincolnshire. Cambridge. Literary Troubles and
Arthur Hallam's Death. Early Years in London. The Begin-
nings of Fame. From *The Princess* to *In Memoriam*. *Maud*.
Idylls of the King. From the *Idylls* to the Dramas. *Queen Mary*
and *Harold*. *The Falcon* and *The Cub*. *The Promise of May*
and *Becket*. From *Tiresias* to *Demeter*. The Closing Years.
The Voice of the Age.

Sixteenth and Cheaper Edition.

TWENTY-FIVE YEARS IN THE SECRET SERVICE.

THE RECOLLECTIONS OF A SPY.

By MAJOR HENRI LE CARON.

With New Preface. 8vo, boards, price 2s. 6d., or cloth 3s. 6d.

Extract from THE TIMES Notice of the First Edition.

" It is of absorbing interest ; and it affords an invaluable key to the dark
history of the great conspiracy which has been the true pivot of our domestic
politics during recent years. It discusses some startling particulars about
certain notorious dynamiters, their confederates, patrons, sympathisers, and
acquaintances. The portraits which the author draws of the Irish-American
leaders, the late associates and paymasters of the Parliamentary party which
has converted the Gladstonians to Home Rule, are vigorous and life-like ; but
the interest inspired by this whole gallery of unscrupulous and venal patriots
pales before that created by the unconscious sketches afforded us of the man
who fought and beat them all."

. *The Library Edition, with Portraits and Facsimiles, 8vo, 14s.,
is still on sale.*

THE KINGDOM OF GOD.

By COUNT LEO TOLSTOY.

Translated from the Russian by CONSTANCE GARNETT.

STORIES OF GOLF.

By PROFESSOR KNIGHT,

Of St. Andrews University;

AND

T. T. OLIPHANT.

Forthcoming Works.

LETTERS OF SAMUEL TAYLOR COLERIDGE.

Edited by Ernest Hartley Coleridge. With Portraits and Illustrations.

MY PARIS NOTEBOOK.

By the Author of "An Englishman in Paris."

VILLIERS DE L'ISLE ADAM:
His Life and Work.

By R. Pontavice de Heussey. Translated from the French by Lady Mary Lovd. With Portrait and Facsimile.

LIFE OF HEINRICH HEINE.

By Richard Garnett, LL.D. With Portrait. Crown 8vo (uniform with the translation of Heine's Works).

LITTLE JOHANNES.

By Frederick van Eeden. Translated from the Dutch by Clara Bell. With an Introduction by Andrew Lang. Illustrated.

⁎ *Also a Large Paper Edition.*

STRAY MEMORIES.

By Ellen Terry. In One Volume. 4to. Illustrated.

A NEW PLAY.

By Björnstjerne Björnson. Translated from the Norwegian.

SONGS ON STONE.

By J. McNeill Whistler. A Series of lithographic drawings in colour by Mr. Whistler, will appear from time to time in parts, under the above title. Each containing four plates. The first issue of 200 copies will be sold at Two Guineas net per part, by Subscription for the Series only.

There will also be issued 50 copies on Japanese paper, signed by the artist, each Five Guineas net.

THE NOVELS OF BJÖRNSTJERNE BJÖRNSON.

UNIFORM EDITION.

The Great Educators.

A Series of Volumes by Eminent Writers, presenting in their entirety "A Biographical History of Education."

The Times. —" A Series of Monographs on ' The Great Educators ' should prove of service to all who concern themselves with the history, theory, and practice of education."

The Speaker. —" There is a promising sound about the title of Mr. Heinemann's new series, ' The Great Educators.' It should help to allay the hunger and thirst for knowledge and culture of the vast multitude of young men and maidens which our educational system turns out yearly, provided at least with an appetite for instruction."

Each subject will form a complete volume, crown 8vo, 5*s.*

Now ready.

ARISTOTLE, and the Ancient Educational Ideals. By THOMAS DAVIDSON, M.A., LL.D.

The Times. —" A very readable sketch of a very interesting subject."

LOYOLA, and the Educational System of the Jesuits. By Rev. THOMAS HUGHES, S.J.

Saturday Review. —" Full of valuable information. . . . . If a schoolmaster would learn how the education of the young can be carried on so as to confer real dignity on those engaged in it, we recommend him to read Mr. Hughes' book."

ALCUIN, and the Rise of the Christian Schools. By Professor ANDREW F. WEST, Ph.D.

FROEBEL, and Education by Self-Activity. By II. COURTHOPE BOWEN, M.A.

ABELARD, and the Origin and Early History of Universities. By JULES GABRIEL COMPAVRÉ, Professor in the Faculty of Toulouse.

In preparation.

ROUSSEAU ; and, Education according to Nature. By PAUL H. HANUS.

HORACE MANN, and Public Education in the United States. By NICHOLAS MURRAY BUTLER, Ph.D.

BELL and LANCASTER, and Public Elementary Education in England. By J. G. FITCH, LL.D., Her Majesty's Inspector of Schools.

Volumes on Herbart, and Modern German Education ; and Pestalozzi ; or, the Friend and Student of Children, to follow.

THE WORKS OF HEINRICH HEINE.

TRANSLATED BY

CHARLES GODFREY LELAND, M.A., F.R.L.S

(HANS BREITMANN).

The Library Edition, in crown 8vo, cloth, at 5*s*. per volume. Each volume of this edition is sold separately. The Cabinet Edition, Vols. I.-VIII. in special binding, boxed, price £2 10*s*. the set. The Large Paper Edition, limited to 100 Numbered Copies, price 15*s*. per volume net, will only be supplied to subscribers for the Complete Work.

The following Volumes, forming

HEINE'S PROSE WORKS,

Are now ready.

I. FLORENTINE NIGHTS, SCHNABELEWOPSKI, THE RABBI OF BACHARACH, and SHAKESPEARE'S MAIDENS AND WOMEN.

II., III. PICTURES OF TRAVEL. 1823-1828. In Two Volumes.

IV. THE SALON. Letters on Art, Music, Popular Life and Politics.

V., VI. GERMANY. In Two Volumes.

VII., VIII. FRENCH AFFAIRS. Letters from Paris 1832 and Lutetia In Two Vols.

Times.—"We can recommend no better medium for making acquaintance at first hand with 'the German Aristophanes' than the works of Heinrich Heine, translated by Charles Godfrey Leland. Mr. Leland manages pretty successfully to preserve the easy grace of the original."

Saturday Review.—"Verily Heinrich Heine and not Jean Paul is *der Einzige* among Germans: and great is the venture of translating him which Mr. Leland has so boldly undertaken, and in which he has for the most part quitted himself so well."

Pall Mall Gazette.—"It is a brilliant performance, both for the quality of the translation of each page and the sustained effort of rendering so many of them. There is really hardly any need to learn German now to appreciate Heine's prose. English literature of this country does not contain much prose more striking, more entertaining, and more thought provoking than these now placed before English readers."

Daily Telegraph.—"Mr. Leland has done his translation in able and scholarly fashion."

In preparation.

THE POETIC WORKS OF HEINRICH HEINE.

The first of which, forming Vol. IX. of the Works, will be

THE BOOK OF SONGS.

Followed by

NEW POEMS.

ATTA TROLL, GERMANY AND ROMANCERO.

LAST POEMS.

*** *Large Paper Edition, limited to 100 Numbered Copies, 15s. each, net. Prospectus on application.*

VICTORIA: Queen and Empress. By JOHN CORDY JEAFFRESON, Author of "The Real Lord Byron," &c. In Two Volumes, 8vo. With Portraits. £1 10s.

DE QUINCEY MEMORIALS. Being Letters and other Records here first Published, with Communications from COLERIDGE, The WORDSWORTHS, HANNAH MORE, PROFESSOR WILSON and others. Edited with Introduction, Notes, and Narrative, by ALEXANDER H. JAPP, LL.D., F.R.S.E. In two volumes, demy 8vo, cloth, with portraits, 30s. net.

RECOLLECTIONS OF MIDDLE LIFE. By FRANCISQUE SARCEY. Translated by E. L. CAREY. In One Volume, 8vo. With Portrait. 10s 6d.

PRINCE BISMARCK. An Historical Biography. By CHARLES LOWE, M.A. With Portraits. Crown 8vo, 6s.

THE FAMILY LIFE OF HEINRICH HEINE. Illustrated by one hundred and twenty-two hitherto unpublished letters addressed by him to different members of his family. Edited by his nephew Baron LUDWIG VON EMBDEN, and translated by CHARLES GODFREY LELAND. In One Volume, 8vo, with 4 Portraits. 12s. 6d.

RECOLLECTIONS OF COUNT LEO TOLSTOY. Together with a Letter to the Women of France on the "Kreutzer Sonata." By C. A. BEHRS. Translated from the Russian by C. E. TURNER, English Lecturer in the University of St. Petersburg. In One Volume, 8vo. With Portrait. 10s. 6d.

THE LIFE OF HENRIK IBSEN. By HENRIK JÆGER. Translated by CLARA BELL. With the Verse done into English from the Norwegian Original by EDMUND GOSSE. Crown 8vo, cloth, 6s.

QUEEN JOANNA I. OF NAPLES, SICILY, AND JERUSALEM; Countess of Provence Forcalquier, and Piedmont. An Essay on her Times. By ST. CLAIR BADDELEY. Imperial 8vo. With Numerous Illustrations. 16s.

THE POSTHUMOUS WORKS OF THOMAS DE QUINCEY. Edited with Introduction and Notes from the Author's Original MSS., by ALEXANDER H. JAPP, LL.D, F.R.S.E., &c. Crown 8vo, cloth, 6s. each.

I. SUSPIRIA DE PROFUNDIS. With other Essays.

II. CONVERSATION AND COLERIDGE. With other Essays.

MR. PUNCH'S POCKET IBSEN. A Collection of some of the Master's best known Dramas, condensed, revised, and slightly rearranged for the benefit of the Earnest Student. By F. ANSTEY, Author of "Vice Versa," "Voces Populi," &c. With Illustrations, reproduced by permission, from Punch, and a new Frontispiece, by Bernard Partridge. 16mo, cloth, 3s. 6d.

FROM WISDOM COURT. By HENRY SETON MERRIMAN and STEPHEN GRAHAM TALLENTYRE. With 30 Illustrations by E. COURBOIN. Crown 8vo, cloth, 3s. 6d.

THE OLD MAIDS' CLUB. By I. ZANGWILL, Author of "The Bachelors' Club." Illustrated by F. H. TOWNSEND. Crown 8vo, cloth, 3s. 6d.

WOMAN—THROUGH A MAN'S EYEGLASS. By MALCOLM C. SALAMAN. With Illustrations by DUDLEY HARDY. Crown 8vo, cloth, 3s. 6d.

THE ART OF TAKING A WIFE. By Professor MANTEGAZZA. Translated from the Italian. Crown 8vo, cloth. [*In the Press.*

GIRLS AND WOMEN. By E. CHESTER. Pott 8vo, cloth, 2s. 6d., or gilt extra, 3s. 6d.

QUESTIONS AT ISSUE. Essays. By EDMUND GOSSE. Crown 8vo, buckram, gilt top, 7s. 6d.

  *** *A Limited Edition on Large Paper, 25s. net.*

GOSSIP IN A LIBRARY. By EDMUND GOSSE, Author of "Northern Studies," &c. Third Edition. Crown 8vo, buckram, gilt top, 7s. 6d.

  *** *A Limited Edition on Large Paper, 25s. net.*

THE ROSE : A Treatise on the Cultivation, History, Family Characteristics, &c., of the Various Groups of Roses. With Accurate Description of the Varieties now Generally Grown. By H. B. ELLWANGER. With an Introduction by GEORGE H ELLWANGER. 12mo, cloth, 5s.

THE GARDEN'S STORY; or, Pleasures and Trials of an Amateur Gardener. By G. H. ELLWANGER. With an Introduction by the Rev. C. WOLLEY DOD. 12mo, cloth, with Illustrations, 5s.

THE GENTLE ART OF MAKING ENEMIES. As pleasingly exemplified in many instances, wherein the serious ones of this earth, carefully exasperated, have been prettily spurred on to indiscretions and unseemliness, while overcome by an undue sense of right. By J. M'NEILL WHISTLER. *A New Edition.* Pott 4to, half-cloth, 10s. 6d.

THE JEW AT HOME. Impressions of a Summer and Autumn Spent with Him in Austria and Russia. By JOSEPH PENNELL. With Illustrations by the Author. 4to, cloth, 5s.

THE NEW EXODUS. A Study of Israel in Russia. By HAROLD FREDERIC. Demy 8vo, Illustrated. 16s.

THE GREAT WAR IN 189—. A Forecast. By Rear-Admiral COLOMB, Col. MAURICE, R.A., Captain MAUDE, ARCHIBALD FORBES, CHARLES LOWE, D. CHRISTIE MURRAY, and F. SCUDAMORE. In One Volume, large 8vo. With numerous Illustrations, 12s. 6d.

IDLE MUSINGS: Essays in Social Mosaic. By E. CONDER GRAY, Author of "Wise Words and Loving Deeds," &c. &c. Crown 8vo, cloth, 6s.

STUDIES OF RELIGIOUS HISTORY. By ERNEST RENAN, late of the French Academy. In One Volume, 8vo, 7s. 6d.

THE ARBITRATOR'S MANUAL. Under the London Chamber of Arbitration. Being a Practical Treatise on the Power and Duties of an Arbitrator, with the Rules and Procedure of the Court of Arbitration, and the Forms. By JOSEPH SEYMOUR SALAMAN, Author of "Trade Marks," etc. Fcap. 8vo, 3s. 6d.

THE COMING TERROR. And other Essays and Letters. By ROBERT BUCHANAN. Second Edition. Demy 8vo, cloth, 12s. 6d.

ARABIC AUTHORS: A Manual of Arabian History and Literature. By F. F. ARBUTHNOT, M.R.A.S., Author of "Early Ideas," "Persian Portraits," &c. 8vo, cloth, 5s.

THE LABOUR MOVEMENT IN AMERICA. By RICHARD T. ELY, Ph.D., Associate in Political Economy, Johns Hopkins University. Crown 8vo, cloth, 5s.

THE SPEECH OF MONKEYS. By Professor R. L. GARNER. Crown 8vo, 7s. 6d.

THE WORD OF THE LORD UPON THE WATERS. Sermons read by His Imperial Majesty the Emperor of Germany, while at Sea on his Voyages to the Land of the Midnight Sun. Composed by Dr. RICHTER, Army Chaplain, and Translated from the German by JOHN R. MCILRAITH. 4to, cloth, 2s. 6d.

THE HOURS OF RAPHAEL, IN OUTLINE. Together with the Ceiling of the Hall where they were originally painted. By MARY E. WILLIAMS. Folio, cloth, £2 2s. net.

THE PASSION PLAY AT OBERAMMERGAU, 1890. By F. W. FARRAR, D.D., F.R.S., Archdeacon and Canon of Westminster, &c. &c. 4to, cloth, 2s. 6d.

THE LITTLE MANX NATION. (Lectures delivered at the Royal Institution, 1891.) By HALL CAINE, Author of "The Bondman," "The Scapegoat," &c. Crown 8vo, cloth, 3s. 6d.; paper, 2s. 6d.

NOTES FOR THE NILE. Together with a Metrical Rendering of the Hymns of Ancient Egypt and of the Precepts of Ptahhotep (the oldest book in the world). By HARDWICKE D. RAWNSLEY, M.A. Imperial 16mo, cloth, 5s.

DENMARK: its History, Topography, Language, Literature, Fine Arts, Social Life, and Finance. Edited by H. WEITEMEYER. Demy 8vo, cloth, with Map, 12s. 6d.

** Dedicated, by permission, to H.R.H. the Princess of Wales.

THE REALM OF THE HABSBURGS. By SIDNEY WHITMAN, Author of "Imperial Germany." In One Volume. Crown 8vo, 7s. 6d.

IMPERIAL GERMANY. A Critical Study of Fact and Character. By SIDNEY WHITMAN. New Edition, Revised and Enlarged. Crown 8vo, cloth 2s. 6d.; paper, 2s.

THE CANADIAN GUIDE-BOOK. Part I. The Tourist's and Sportsman's Guide to Eastern Canada and Newfoundland, including full descriptions of Routes, Cities, Points of Interest, Summer Resorts, Fishing Places, &c., in Eastern Ontario, The Muskoka District, The St. Lawrence Region, The Lake St. John Country, The Maritime Provinces, Prince Edward Island, and Newfoundland. With an Appendix giving Fish and Game Laws, and Official Lists of Trout and Salmon Rivers and their Lessees. By CHARLES G. D. ROBERTS, Professor of English Literature in King's College, Windsor, N.S. With Maps and many Illustrations. Crown 8vo. limp cloth, 6s.

Part II. **WESTERN CANADA.** Including the Peninsula and Northern Regions of Ontario, the Canadian Shores of the Great Lakes, the Lake of the Woods Region, Manitoba and "The Great North-West," The Canadian Rocky Mountains and National Park British Columbia, and Vancouver Island. By ERNEST INGERSOLL. With Maps and many Illustrations.. Crown 8vo, limp cloth, 6s.

THE GUIDE-BOOK TO ALASKA AND THE NORTH-WEST COAST, including the Shores of Washington, British Columbia, South-Eastern Alaska, the Aleutian and the Seal Islands, the Behring and the Arctic Coasts. By E. R. SCIDMORE. With Maps and many Illustrations. Crown 8vo, limp cloth, 6s.

THE GENESIS OF THE UNITED STATES. A Narrative of the Movement in England, 1605–1616, which resulted in the Plantation of North America by Englishmen, disclosing the Contest between England and Spain for the Possession of the Soil now occupied by the United States of America; set forth through a series of Historical Manuscripts now first printed, together with a Re-Issue of Rare Contemporaneous Tracts, accompanied by Bibliographical Memoranda, Notes, and Brief Biographies. Collected, Arranged, and Edited by ALEXANDER BROWN, F.R.H.S. With 100 Portraits, Maps, and Plans. In two volumes. Royal 8vo, buckram, £3 13s 6d.

Fiction.

NEW THREE-VOLUME NOVELS.

THE HEAVENLY TWINS. By SARAH GRAND, Author of "Ideala," &c. Fourth Thousand.

THE COUNTESS RADNA. By W. E. NORRIS, Author of " Matrimony," &c.

AS A MAN IS ABLE. By DOROTHY LEIGHTON.

A COMEDY OF MASKS. By ERNEST DOWSON and ARTHUR MOORE.

THE HOYDEN. By Mrs. HUNGERFORD.

A SUPERFLUOUS WOMAN. [*In preparation.*]

BENEFITS FORGOT. By WOLCOTT BALESTIER. [*In preparation.*]

A DAUGHTER OF MUSIC. By G. COLMORE, Author of "A Conspiracy of Silence," &c. [*In preparation.*]

THE SURRENDER OF MARGARET BELLAR-MINE. By ADELINE SERGEANT, Author of " No Saint," &c. [*In preparation.*]

A NEW NOVEL. By HALL CAINE. [*In preparation.*]

A NEW NOVEL. By W. E. NORRIS. [*In preparation.*]

NEW ONE-VOLUME NOVELS.

THE KING OF THE SCHNORRERS, AND OTHER GROTESQUES. By I. ZANGWILL. [*In preparation.*]

THE LAST SENTENCE. By MAXWELL GRAY, Author of " The Silence of Dean Maitland," &c. [*In preparation.*]

A BATTLE AND A BOY. By BLANCHE WILLIS HOWARD. Author of "Guenn," &c. 6s. [*In preparation.*]

MR. BAILEY MARTIN. By PERCY WHITE. [*In preparation.*]

THE RECIPE FOR DIAMONDS. By C. J. CUTLIFFE HYNE. [*In preparation.*]

MOTHER'S HANDS, and DUST. By BJÖRNSTJERNE BJÖRNSON. [*In preparation.*]

JOANNA TRAIL, SPINSTER. By ANNIE E. HOLDSWORTH. [*In preparation.*]

Fiction.

Six Shilling Volumes.

APPASSIONATA: A Musician's Story. By ELSA D'ESTERRE-KEELING. 6s.

FROM THE FIVE RIVERS. By FLORA ANNIE STEEL, Author of " Miss Stuart's Legacy." Crown 8vo, cloth, 6s.

RELICS. By FRANCES MACNAB. Crown 8vo, cloth, 6s.

IDEALA. By SARAH GRAND, Author of " The Heavenly Twins." Fifth Edition. Crown 8vo, cloth, 6s.

THE TOWER OF TADDEO. By OUIDA, Author of " Two Little Wooden Shoes," &c. New Edition. Crown 8vo, cloth, Illustrated. 6s.

CHILDREN OF THE GHETTO. By I. ZANGWILL, Author of " The Old Maids' Club," &c. New Edition, with Glossary. Crown 8vo, cloth, 6s.

THE PREMIER AND THE PAINTER. A Fantastic Romance. By I. ZANGWILL and LOUIS COWEN. Third Edition. Crown 8vo, cloth, 6s.

THE NAULAHKA. A Tale of West and East. By RUDYARD KIPLING and WOLCOTT BALESTIER. Second Edition. Crown 8vo, cloth, 6s.

AVENGED ON SOCIETY. By H. F. WOOD, Author of " The Englishman of the Rue Cain," " The Passenger from Scotland Yard." Crown 8vo. Cloth, 6s.

THE O'CONNORS OF BALLINAHINCH. By Mrs. HUNGERFORD, Author of " Molly Bawn," &c. Crown 8vo. Cloth, 6s.

PASSION THE PLAYTHING. A Novel. By R. MURRAY GILCHRIST. Crown 8vo, cloth, 6s.

Five Shilling Volumes.

THE SECRET OF NARCISSE. By EDMUND GOSSE. Crown 8vo, buckram, 5s.

THE PENANCE OF PORTIA JAMES. By TASMA, Author of " Uncle Piper of Piper's Hill," &c. Crown 8vo, cloth, 5s.

INCONSEQUENT LIVES. A Village Chronicle. By J. H. PEARCE, Author of " Esther Pentreath," &c. Crown 8vo, cloth, 5s.

A QUESTION OF TASTE. By MAARTEN MAARTENS, Author of " An Old Maid's Love," &c. Crown 8vo, cloth, 5s.

COME LIVE WITH ME AND BE MY LOVE. By ROBERT BUCHANAN, Author of " The Moment After," " The Coming Terror," &c. Crown 8vo, cloth, 5s.

VANITAS. By VERNON LEE, Author of " Hauntings," &c. Crown 8vo, cloth, 5s.

THE DOMINANT SEVENTH. A Musical Story. By KATE ELIZABETH CLARKE. Crown 8vo, cloth, 5s.

Heinemann's International Library.

Edited by EDMUND GOSSE.

New Review.—" If you have any pernicious remnants of literary chauvinism I hope it will not survive the series of foreign classics of which Mr. William Heinemann, aided by Mr. Edmund Gosse, is publishing translations to the great contentment of all lovers of literature."

Each Volume has an Introduction specially written by the Editor.

Price, in paper covers, 2*s.* 6*d.* each, or cloth, 3*s.* 6*d.*

IN GOD'S WAY. From the Norwegian of BJÖRNSTJERNE BJÖRNSON.

PIERRE AND JEAN. From the French of GUY DE MAUPASSANT.

THE CHIEF JUSTICE. From the German of KARL EMIL FRANZOS, Author of "For the Right," &c.

WORK WHILE YE HAVE THE LIGHT. From the Russian of Count LEO TOLSTOY.

FANTASY. From the Italian of MATILDE SERAO.

FROTH. From the Spanish of Don ARMANDO PALACIO-VALDÉS.

FOOTSTEPS OF FATE. From the Dutch of LOUIS COUPERUS.

PEPITA JIMÉNEZ. From the Spanish of JUAN VALERA.

THE COMMODORE'S DAUGHTERS. From the Norwegian of JONAS LIE.

THE HERITAGE OF THE KURTS. From the Norwegian of BJÖRNSTJERNE BJÖRNSON.

LOU. From the German of BARON ALEXANDER VON ROBERTS.

DOÑA LUZ. From the Spanish of JUAN VALERA.

THE JEW. From the Polish of JOSEPH IGNATIUS KRASZEWSKI.

UNDER THE YOKE. From the Bulgarian of IVAN VAZOFF.

FAREWELL LOVE. From the Italian of MATILDE SERAO.
[In preparation.

A COMMON STORY. From the Russian of GONCHAROFF.

ABSALOM'S HAIR. From the Norwegian of BJÖRNSTERNE BJÖRNSON.

Popular 3s. 6d. Novels.

16 MR. WILLIAM HEINEMANN'S LIST.

Popular 3s. 6d. Novels.

CAPT'N DAVY'S HONEYMOON, The Blind Mother, and The Last Confession. By HALL CAINE, Author of "The Bondman," "The Scapegoat" &c. Sixth Thousand.

THE SCAPEGOAT. By HALL CAINE, Author of "The Bondman," &c. Nineteenth Thousand.

THE BONDMAN. A New Saga. By HALL CAINE. Twenty-third Thousand.

DESPERATE REMEDIES. By THOMAS HARDY, Author of "Tess of the D'Urbervilles," &c.

A LITTLE MINX. By ADA CAMBRIDGE, Author of "A Marked Man," &c.

A MARKED MAN: Some Episodes in his Life. By ADA CAMBRIDGE, Author of "Two Years' Time," "A Mere Chance," &c.

THE THREE MISS KINGS. By ADA CAMBRIDGE, Author of "A Marked Man."

NOT ALL IN VAIN. By ADA CAMBRIDGE, Author of "A Marked Man," "The Three Miss Kings," &c.

A KNIGHT OF THE WHITE FEATHER. By TASMA, Author of "The Penance of Portia James," "Uncle Piper of Piper's Hill," &c.

UNCLE PIPER OF PIPER'S HILL. By TASMA. New Popular Edition.

THE COPPERHEAD. By HAROLD FREDERIC, Author of "The Return of the O Mahony," &c. [*In the Press.*

THE RETURN OF THE O'MAHONY. By HAROLD FREDERIC, Author of "In the Valley," &c. With Illustrations.

IN THE VALLEY. By HAROLD FREDERIC, Author of "The Lawton Girl," "Seth's Brother's Wife," &c. With Illustrations.

PRETTY MISS SMITH. By FLORENCE WARDEN, Author of "The House on the Marsh," "A Witch of the Hills," &c.

THE STORY OF A PENITENT SOUL. Being the Private Papers of Mr. Stephen Dart, late Minister at Lynnbridge, in the County of Lincoln. By ADELINE SERGEANT, Author of "No Saint," &c.

NOR WIFE, NOR MAID. By Mrs. HUNGERFORD, Author of "Molly Bawn," &c.

MAMMON. A Novel. By Mrs. ALEXANDER, Author of "The Wooing O't," &c.

DAUGHTERS OF MEN. By HANNAH LYNCH, Author of "The Prince of the Glades," &c.

A ROMANCE OF THE CAPE FRONTIER. By BERTRAM MITFORD, Author of "Through the Zulu Country," &c.

'TWEEN SNOW AND FIRE. A Tale of the Kafir War of 1877. By BERTRAM MITFORD.

Popular 3s. 6d. Novels.

ORIOLE'S DAUGHTER. By JESSIE FOTHERGILL, Author of "The First Violin," &c.

THE MASTER OF THE MAGICIANS. By ELIZABETH STUART PHELPS and HERBERT D. WARD.

THE HEAD OF THE FIRM. By Mrs. RIDDELL, Author of "George Geith," "Maxwell Drewett," &c.

ACCORDING TO ST. JOHN. By AMÉLIE RIVES, Author of "The Quick or the Dead."

KITTY'S FATHER. By FRANK BARRETT, Author of "The Admirable Lady Biddy Fane," &c.

DONALD MARCY. By ELIZABETH STUART PHELPS, Author of "The Gates Ajar," &c.

PERCHANCE TO DREAM, and other Stories. By MARGARET S. BRISCOE.

WRECKERS AND METHODISTS. Cornish Stories. By H. D. LOWRY.

IN THE DWELLINGS OF SILENCE. A Romance of Russia. By WALKER KENNEDY.

THE AVERAGE WOMAN. By WOLCOTT BALESTIER. With an Introduction by HENRY JAMES.

THE ATTACK ON THE MILL, and other Sketches of War. By EMILE ZOLA. With an essay on the short stories of M. Zola by Edmund Gosse.

WRECKAGE, and other Stories. By HUBERT CRACKANTHORPE.

MADEMOISELLE MISS, and other Stories. By HENRY HARLAND, Author of "Mea Culpa," &c.

TRUE RICHES. By FRANÇOIS COPPÉE. With an Introduction by T. P. O'CONNOR. [In the Press.

LOS CERRITOS. A Romance of the Modern Time. By GERTRUDE FRANKLIN ATHERTON, Author of "Hermia Suydam," and "What Dreams may Come."

A MODERN MARRIAGE. By the Marquise CLARA LANZA.

Popular Shilling Books.

MADAME VALERIE. By F. C. PHILIPS, Author of "As in a Looking-Glass," &c.

THE MOMENT AFTER: A Tale of the Unseen. By ROBERT BUCHANAN.

CLUES; or, Leaves from a Chief Constable's Note-Book. By WILLIAM HENDERSON, Chief Constable of Edinburgh.

Dramatic Literature.

THE MASTER BUILDER. A Play in Three Acts. By HENRIK IBSEN. Translated from the Norwegian by EDMUND GOSSE and WILLIAM ARCHER. Small 4to, with Portrait, 5s. Popular Edition, paper, 1s. Also a Limited Large Paper Edition, 21s. net.

HEDDA GABLER: A Drama in Four Acts. By HENRIK IBSEN. Translated from the Norwegian by EDMUND GOSSE. Small 4to, cloth, with Portrait, 5s. Vaudeville Edition, paper, 1s. Also a Limited Large Paper Edition, 21s. net.

BRAND. A Drama in Verse. By HENRIK IBSEN. Translated from the Norwegian by C. H. HERFORD. Cloth, 5s.

THE PRINCESSE MALEINE: A Drama in Five Acts (Translated by Gerard Harry), and THE INTRUDER: A Drama in One Act. By MAURICE MAETERLINCK. With an Introduction by HALL CAINE, and a Portrait of the Author. Small 4to, cloth, 5s.

THE FRUITS OF ENLIGHTENMENT: A Comedy in Four Acts. By Count LYOF TOLSTOY. Translated from the Russian by E. J. DILLON. With Introduction by A. W. PINERO. Small 4to, with Portrait, 5s.

KING ERIK. A Tragedy. By EDMUND GOSSE. A Re-issue with a Critical Introduction by Mr. THEODORE WATTS. Fcap. 8vo, boards, 5s. net.

THE DRAMA: ADDRESSES. By HENRY IRVING. With Portrait by J. McN. Whistler. Second Edition. Fcap. 8vo. 3s. 6d.

SOME INTERESTING FALLACIES OF THE Modern Stage. An Address delivered to the Playgoers' Club at St. James's Hall, on Sunday, 6th December, 1891. By HERBERT BEERBOHM TREE. Crown 8vo, sewed, 6d. net.

THE PLAYS OF ARTHUR W. PINERO. With Introductory Notes by MALCOLM C. SALAMAN. 16mo, Paper Covers, 1s. 6d.; or Cloth, 2s. 6d. each.

   I. **THE TIMES:** A Comedy in Four Acts. With a Preface by the Author.

  II. **THE PROFLIGATE:** A Play in Four Acts. With Portrait of the Author, after J. MORDECAI.

 III. **THE CABINET MINISTER:** A Farce in Four Acts.

  IV. **THE HOBBY HORSE:** A Comedy in Three Acts.

   V. **LADY BOUNTIFUL:** A Play in Four Acts.

  VI. **THE MAGISTRATE:** A Farce in Three Acts.

 VII. **DANDY DICK:** A Farce in Three Acts.

VIII. **SWEET LAVENDER.** A Drama in Three Acts.

  IX. **THE SCHOOLMISTRESS.** A Farce in Three Acts.

To be followed by **The Second Mrs. Tanqueray, The Weaker Sex, Lords and Commons,** and **The Squire.**

Poetry.

TENNYSON'S GRAVE. By St. Clair Baddeley. 8vo, paper, 1s.

LOVE SONGS OF ENGLISH POETS, 1500—1800. With Notes by Ralph H. Caine. Fcap. 8vo, rough edges, 3s. 6d.
  . *Large Paper Edition, limited to 100 Copies,* 10s. 6d. *net.*

IVY AND PASSION FLOWER: Poems. By Gerard Bendall, Author of "Estelle," &c. &c. 12mo, cloth, 3s. 6d.
Scotsman.—"Will be read with pleasure."
Musical World.—"The poems are delicate specimens of art, graceful and polished.'

VERSES. By Gertrude Hall. 12mo, cloth, 3s. 6d.
Manchester Guardian.—"Will be welcome to every lover of poetry who takes it up."

IDYLLS OF WOMANHOOD. By C. Amy Dawson. Fcap. 8vo, gilt top, 5s.

Heinemann's Scientific Handbooks.

MANUAL OF BACTERIOLOGY. By A. B. Griffiths, Ph.D., F.R.S. (Edin.), F.C.S. Crown 8vo, cloth, Illustrated. 7s. 6d.
Pharmaceutical Journal.—"The subject is treated more thoroughly and completely than in any similar work published in this country. . . . . It should prove a useful aid to pharmacists, and all others interested in the increasingly important subject of which it treats, and particularly so to those possessing little or no previous knowledge concerning the problems of micro-biology."

MANUAL OF ASSAYING GOLD, SILVER, COPPER, and Lead Ores. By Walter Lee Brown, B.Sc. Revised, Corrected, and considerably Enlarged, with a chapter on the Assaying of Fuel, &c. By A. B. Griffiths, Ph.D., F.R.S. (Edin.), F.C.S. Crown 8vo, cloth, Illustrated, 7s. 6d.
Colliery Guardian.—"A delightful and fascinating book."
Financial World.—"The most complete and practical manual on everything which concerns assaying of all which have come before us."

GEODESY. By J. Howard Gore. Crown 8vo, cloth, Illustrated, 5s.
St. James's Gazette.—"The book may be safely recommended to those who desire to acquire an accurate knowledge of Geodesy."
Science Gossip.—"It is the best we could recommend to all geodetic students. It is full and clear, thoroughly accurate, and up to date in all matters of earth-measurements."

THE PHYSICAL PROPERTIES OF GASES. By Arthur L. Kimball, of the Johns Hopkins University. Crown 8vo, cloth, Illustrated, 5s.
Chemical News.—"The man of culture who wishes for a general and accurate acquaintance with the physical properties of gases, will find in Mr. Kimball's work just what he requires."

HEAT AS A FORM OF ENERGY. By Professor R. H. Thurston, of Cornell University. Crown 8vo, cloth, Illustrated, 5s.
Manchester Examiner.—"Bears out the character of its predecessors for careful and correct statement and deduction under the light of the most recent discoveries."

THE NORTH AMERICAN REVIEW.

The London Office of this old-established Review has been removed to 21 Bedford Street, where copies can be obtained regularly on publication.   Price 2s. 6d.

THE NEW REVIEW.

With the commencement of the New Year this well-known Magazine will be published by Mr. WM. HEINEMANN.   There will be no change in the editorial department, which will remain under the direction of Mr. ARCHIBALD GROVE, M.P.

LONDON:
WILLIAM HEINEMANN,
21 BEDFORD STREET, W.C.